Ray Of Sunshine

Wilma Bey

Contents

CHAPTER 1	1
CHAPTER 2	3
CHAPTER 3	8
CHAPTER 4	15
CHAPTER 5	20
CHAPTER 6	25
CHAPTER 7	33
CHAPTER 8	41
CHAPTER 9	51
CHAPTER 10	59
CHAPTER 11	68
CHAPTER 12	77
CHAPTER 13	88
CHAPTER 14	94
CHAPTER 15	102

CHAPTER 16 112

CHAPTER 17 117

CHAPTER 1

I t was one of those days in the orphanage where everyone is busy trying to look pretty for adoption. While am in my room clutching on to my best friend penny (panda stuffie) trying to block out all that is happening around me. Ohh I forgot to introduce myself my name is Mia, am 4 years old I have lived in this orphanage my whole life where I get bullied for not being pretty or slim by some of the kids in the orphanage. Lila the leader and her minions Simon, Kylie, Emily, Jake and Rose they never missed a chance to remind me how ugly I am or how fat I am. Mrs Johnson the owner of the orphanage bully us verbally and sometimes it gets physical, well I on the other hand am always her scapegoat when it gets physical, she always mocks me on how ugly I am and for not getting adopted for being so.

So today it's an adoption day where parents come for adoption, I really hate this day because I get locked up in my room because Mrs Johnson doesn't want the parents to see my ugly face.I hug my stuffie so tight like my life depends on it when I heard some foot steps I know I haven't done anything wrong yet but sometimes I get scold for others doings. When the door open I heard Mrs Johnson " hey fatty get up and get dress better make sure you look presentable because I don't want you to disgrace me today, maybe you will get adopted or maybe not because I wonder who would like to adopt someone like you as a child" said that and walks away laughing like a maniac "okay Mrs Johnson" I said I walked up to my small closet and took out my best outfit and wore it, when I was done I went downstairs to look for Mrs Johnson. I saw her standing and talking to two men in black suits, when she saw me she glared at me and forced a smile "Mia darling come here, wait for me in the waiting room with the others".I walked into the room what I saw made my heart drop and the hope I had was long gone because Lila, Emily and Rose were looking gorgeous and stunning as always when I looked at my outfit I was no match to theirs.

Lila was the first to look up "well isn't it the ugly duckling" she said and laughed. " What's the fatty doing here" Rose said making a disgust look.E mily laughed " girls look at her outfit seriously does she think she's getting adopted looking like that" they all started laughing and making fun of me and my outfit, I felt my eyes started to get glossy but soon blinks it away when the door knob turned.

Mrs Johnson walks in with the two men I saw her standing at the door with "girls this is Mr Alexander DeLuca he's here looking for a baby girl to adopt and that's his PA and also best friend James Smith, well one of you is going to be the lucky girl but before that each one of you will have 15 mins talk with him in a separate run to know which one he wants to adopt" the girls squealed well I didn't because my head was down I was overwhelmed with the fact that am gonna be in the same room with this two men. My gaze was down but I can get this feeling that someone was staring at me when I looked up I saw the most beautiful blue eyes that I have ever seen even though I have one, the one staring at me was none other than Mr DeLuca.I clutched onto penny tightly feeling so overwhelmed, maybe I will get adopted and maybe I will not because am ugly and fat on like the rest.

CHAPTER 2

It was a hectic day. I came back from work, freshen up, have dinner and went to bed because am so tired.

The next day

Beep! Beep! I groan when I heard the sound of the alarm. Gosh I need to work on my sleeping schedule I thought. Walked into the washroom do my morning routine, came back to the room and sat on the bed. Took my phone to see many messages from my parents and siblings some from business partners while some from James. I view his messages

J: Hey man hope you thought about what I said yesterday, if you're up for it I will be in your house in 2 hours.Seriously I thought.

A: okay J. I send and sighed

I started to think about what he said yesterday at the office.

Flashback..

I was busy trying to complete some of the remaining work I have even being the CEO of a famous company I have to try do some work that my PA can't do for me. While I was busy working James my best friend and also PA burst into my cabin.

He entered hold two cups of coffee in his hand, gave one to me and started to sip on the other. " Hey man still doing the work" I sighed." Yeah I have to finish this before going home today, I want to take a day off tomorrow am tired honestly".

I said and he let out a chuckle" man you have to live a little bit stop stressing yourself, so what about the adoption I have heard about you searching for another orphanage since the couple of orphanages you visited". He said

" Man those kids from those orphanages are spoiled brats, seriously man I was shocked when one of them said she wants her own private jet she was just what 5 years old dude" I said and he started laughing.

I glared at him"it's so funny, but I heard about one orphanage named Mary Johnson orphanage. You gotta check that orphanage Alex maybe you're going to get your baby girl there, infact I will escort you there to help you choose the right one" he checked his watch and said I gotta go man see you tomorrow but please think about it I don't wanna see you have a long face every single day".

I sighed " okay J, I will think about only this orphanage after it no more". I said

" See you tomorrow or Melody will kill me bye". He said and left. I laughed at his silliness.

End of flashback

After I thought about what he said I went downstairs to have breakfast. I walked into the dinning room I saw one of the house keepers "good morning Mrs Williams" i said I know what's coming after saying so.

She glared at me "Alexander DeLuca how many times would I tell you to stop calling me Mrs Williams and to call me Celia" she said and I laughed.

"You know I can't call you Celia Mrs Williams, what's for breakfast" I said rubbing my hands.

"It's pancakes, waffles, scrambled eggs and bacon" she said with a smile.

I told her what I want to eat, she served me and left .After having my breakfast I went back to my room and started to work after, an hour and a half I heard the door bell ring. Well that must be James, I close the laptop and change into a suit and went downstairs to see James talking to Mrs Williams and laughing.

He's also wearing a suit "Hey J, how are you doing" I said

He smiled " am good man, you ready" he asked

" Yep I'm let's do this" I said.

" Bye Mrs Williams" we said

"Bye dearies, hoping to see you guys coming back into this house with a baby in your arms and good luck" she said and waved at us.

" We will and thanks" I hope and walked out.

We entered the car " so it's gonna take us at least 20 minutes to reach there so make yourself comfortable" J said

" Okay J, maybe today you're going to be an uncle" I said

He squealed like a girl" I hope so man" he said and I laughed at his silliness.

After 20 minutes we reached the orphanage. It was crowded with different people, I assumed parents who wants to adopt a kid too like me.

We walked into the orphanage, kids of different age running and playing with each other or talking to some parents. James walked up to a woman in her mid forties and start talking to her, she looked up saw me and smile waving her hand she muttered hey and I waved back.

After some talking the came up to me " Alex this is Mrs Mary Johnson the owner of the orphanage that I told you about on our way here" J said and I nod

"Hello Mr DeLuca, am glad that you came to this orphanage looking for the perfect little girl, hoping you will get one here" she said and smiled

" Looking forward to Mrs Johnson" I said.

" Well right this way gentle men follow me, I heard that you were looking for a little girl between the age of 5-3 right" she said and I nod.

" So I have 4 girls within that age which I think one of them will be your match sir and....." She was interrupted by the sound of little foot steps.

It became closer and closer what I saw made my heart melt. A little girl clutching onto her stuffie looking so cute she was staring at us with big wide eyes. Wow! she has the most amazing blue eyes like mine. She looked down when she saw Mrs Johnson glaring at her.

I frowned why would she glared at her like that. Still looking at her " Mia darling, come here wait for me in the waiting room with the others" she said to the little girl.

She walked slowly to us like she's scared or something. I deepen the frown on my face.

She turned to us " well gentle men in this room there are 4 girls which I told you about, you going to have to talk to each one of them in a separate room for 15 minutes okay" she said and smiled we nod.

She claps her hand and turned the door knob

We walked into the room, I saw 3 girls wearing dresses and were talking and playing with each other. While the girl that walked into the room when we were outside who I got to know her name Mia, was having tears in her eyes but blinks it away in a few seconds.

Mrs Johnson clapped her hands which got the girls attention "girls this is Mr Alexander DeLuca he's here looking for a baby girl to adopt and that's his PA and also best friend James Smith, well one of you is going to be the lucky girl but before that each one of you will have 15 mins talk with him in a separate run to know which one he wants to adopt" they squealed but Mia didn't and I frowned at that.

Is she not happy or what I thought. I kept staring at her until she looked up and saw me staring but quickly looked down again clutching onto to her stuffie like her life depends on it.

Well interesting she's shy but I like her already. Maybe just maybe I could have her as my princess who I will spoil rotten and cherish forever.

I only hope she will accept me but before that I have to talk to her and know her a little bit in those 15 minutes.

CHAPTER 3

Sitting in the room waiting for the next girl, he sigh. The two girls he talked to in those 30 minutes was exhausting, he couldn't believe he ears on how they talk to him they're so disrespectful and so spoiled. They haven't given him a chance to talk to ask them, they have talking about their selves and what they want from him. When he tried to ask question they will interrupt and say something else. Two more to go he said to his friend.

The next girl came in with her head down, standing by the door fiddling her fingers, she seems nervous she inhaled deeply trying to calm her nerves. Took a seat across him, slowly she looked up and saw those blue eyes staring at her, quickly she lowered her gaze.

He cleared his throat which got her attention again she looked up.

"Hello beautiful" he said

She looked at him eyes wide, did he just called her beautiful. She blush as she thought at being called beautiful.

"Hello" she said quietly

She's not like the others, she's shy and polite.

"Um... so what's your name" he ask even though he knew her name he wants to hear it from her.

"Mia sir" she said still fiddling her hand.

"So you already know my name am Alexander DeLuca and also my friend James here" he said pointing at the man beside him, she nod.

"So Mia who's your friend" he asked his gaze on her stuffie.

She smiled "she's penny my best friend" clutching onto it.

"What's your favorite color" James asked

" Purple"she replied

"Your favorite snack" he asked again

"Gummy bears" she replied

He kept on asking her some questions while Alex was studying her he saw how she's becoming more comfortable with them and was less tensed as she was before.

"So Mia what do you think of Alex and do you want him to be your new daddy" he asked her which got his attention.

He was curious on what she's going to say about him.

" He's nice but he's kinda scary" she mumbled the last part but he heard, he chuckled at being called scary.

" So you think am scary princess" he said with a smirk looking at her, she was shocked he heard her.

" I.... no.... am" she stammered, she started panicking she thought he was mad at her.

He saw she's panicking, he rushed over to her to calm her " hey, hey baby girl am just kidding" she calmed down a bit but he kept on rubbing her back.

" Okay thanks" she said, he nods and went back to his seat.

" So Mia how did you get that bruise on your forehead" he asked she tenses at the question, she thought she hide it with her hair but she guess it didn't work.

" I fell" she said it was half true, the atmosphere in the room was getting more tense.

" May I go now" she said, looking up to see why he didn't reply back .

" Yeah you may go" said James

Alex didn't believe her because the bruise wasn't looking as she said that's why he didn't reply he was in his on world of trance on what will cause that nasty bruise on her forehead, he noticed it when she first came into the room but didn't say anything until she's comfortable enough with them in order to answer but he wasn't satisfied with her answer.

Is someone abusing her or what he thought, the came back to reality on hearing the door shut.

He turned to him friend " what do you think of her and that bruise I don't believe her man" he said

" She's so cute I really like her she's not like the others and that bruise am with you" James said

Alex sigh " I want her" James looked at him shocked he knows that she caught his friends eyes but wasn't sure if he's gonna adopt her.

" But still have one more girl" he said.

" Whatever man but she's the one I want" Alex said

After talking to the last girl, they went back to Mrs Johnson's office to talk to her on who he decided to adopt. She was shocked when she heard that it's Mia.

" But Mr DeLuca do you want to adopt that brat she's so..." Mrs Johnson said, he gave a stern glare with shut her up

" Yeah she's the one I want is there any problem" he said give her the same glare.

" I... n..no sir" she replied

" I thought so" he said

" So I will be with you in a moment lemme inform my assistant to help her pack her bag" she said rushing out.

" Am so happy for you man" James said smile

" I know right she's so adorable J I really like her a lot I hope she will warm up to me and accept me as her father" Alex said sighting.

" Xander don't worry I know she will she's a sweetheart" James said patting his back

Mrs Johnson came and gave them the papers to sign for the adoption. He signed and asked where Mia is. She said she's going to meet them at the front door.

Mean while was happy that she's living that hell whole. She was engrossed in packing her back she doesn't have many clothes. She packed her clothes in her small bag pack. She was about to leave the room when Lila came in with her minions.

" Oh so he picked the ugly duckling" said Rose

" I don't know what he sees in her she's so fat and so ugly argh" Emily said

Lila laughed " what a pity don't be so excited fatty when he sees how useless you are he will come back and dump you here again. Don't worry girls maybe he's not in his rightful mind that why he didn't see what you are saying but when he does he's going to get rid of her" they laughed walking away.

Mia sat down and cried her heart out, then came in Miss Lisa she's the only one who's not mean to her in the orphanage. She always tries to cheer her up when she's sad.

" Honey why are you crying" she asked Mia

She told her what happened with glossy eyes.

" Oh poor baby don't take what they said to heart they are just jealous of you because you're beautiful" she told her .

" Okay" Mia said

" So let's go your new daddy is so eager to take you home with him" Miss Lisa said

" Really"

"Yes Mia so stop shedding does tears princesses don't cry" she said smiling at her

She got up and went to the washroom wash her face " okay am ready now miss Lisa" she said clutching onto penny.

They went to the front door and saw Mrs Johnson and Alex waiting for her.

Miss Lisa bend towards her and whispered" baby he's a good man please try and give him a chance don't shut him out okay try and warm up to him he's going to take good care of you. I can see it in his eyes that he already adores you Mia" saying that Mia looked up and saw Alex looking at her lovingly.

" I will miss Lisa" said Mia

" You ready to go princess" he asked and she nod

Mrs. Johnson was glaring at her

" Mia darling aren't you going to give me a goodbye hug" she said

Mia on hearing that she tenses, Alex frowned as she tenses because she tightened her hold on him as they were holding hands.

He picked her up she immediately put her face in the crook of his neck clutching his shirt and penny finding comfort she sighed.

" Mrs Johnson it's nice meeting you, we will leaving now as you can see she's tired and thank you" Alex said after hearing soft snores coming from Mia he assumed she's sleeping

" Okay and thanks too" she said and he smiled

He went over to his car and place Mia gently on the car seat trying not to wake her up. He smiled when he succeed and peck her forehead she smiled in her sleep.

" Please take care of her, she had gone through a lot" miss Lisa who came running to Alex said

She saw the confusion on his face and said" she will tell you when she's comfortable don't worry" and with that she walked away.

Alex sighed as he entered his car and sped up to his house, grining like he won a lottery.

He parked as he saw Mia still sleeping. He carefully took her out of the car seat.

As he entered the house Celia came up to him as she squealed like a teenager" is she the one" she asked

" Yes she is my princess" he said gesturing her to keep quiet as she's sleeping.

" Okay take her up to your room i will go make my famous chocolate chip cookies for her" she said heading towards the kitchen

Alex shakes his head amused on the way she's behaving.

He took her to his room, placing her on his bed he place a kiss on her cheek, nose and forehead making his lips lingering for some seconds where her bruise is before saying " sleep tight princess I won't let anyone hurt you again am gonna protect you for the rest of my life I love you" he peck her forehead again and left his room to check on Celia.

Hello guys, what do you think of this chapter?Hope you like it.Please if you are liking this story pls vote

CHAPTER 4

Waking up in an unfamiliar place, Mia panic but soon recall that she was adopted by Mr. Handsome a small smile makes it way to her lips but it vanishes when she thought maybe he will hurt, he is just being friendly before he starts it. She came out of her thoughts when the door knob turned, she went under the covers to hide started shaking and crying quietly. Alex frowned when he saw how she's shaking badly, he immediately remove the covers she flinch a little when he placed his hand on her shoulder.

His heart felt like it's breaking into million he just met her a few hours ago but he really adores he can't see her in tears he hates it because it breaks his heart to see her like that.

He gently lift he chin up her eyes are red and also her nose because of how much she cried, his eyes softened as he sees her condition "baby why are you crying, what's wrong, princess are you hurt, did you had a nightmare, baby girl please talk to me" he said her but she kept sniffling, she couldn't reply.

He just hugged her like his life depends on it or someone's gonna snatch her out of his arms.

"I got scawred when I woke up and you were not there" she replied, he chuckled on how she said the scared in her baby voice.

He cooed at her cuteness "aww was my baby scared when she didn't see her dada close to her when she woke up" she nod and kept sniffling burying her face in the crook of his neck.

"Am so sorry baby daddy's gonna make it up to you and won't let that happen again. Princess I was scared when I saw you shaking & crying I thought u had a nightmare or you're hurt" he kissed he hair repeatedly & apologizing for not being by her side.

She was in her own thoughts again, he really cares about me, he's even saying sorry for something that's not even his fault and nobody hugs me it's only miss Lisa that has done that and I have never felt safe with anyone until him. I should give him a chance before he starts hurting me am gonna enjoy his endearment and affection for now. She thought and smile.

She wiped her tears saying "it's okay Mr Alex" he just hummed nuzzling into her hair.

"So baby what do you wanna do, take a bath or eat dinner" he asked tickling her.

She was giggling "take a bath" he cooed "okay baby girl bath it is" saying that her stomach growled.

"But I think someone's hungry are you sure you wanna take a bath before dinner" she blushed and nod her head , he chuckled and went into the washroom to set up a bath full of bubbles for her.

She went under the covers giggling hiding from him. He saw what she did and he chuckled "where's my baby girl I can't find her, did the fairies took her away from me" he said with a sad & worried voice.

She heard him and was feeling guilty for making him worried and sad, she immediately came out of the covers and hugged him from behind " I sowwie Mr Alex no fairwes took me" she said in a sad voice.

"Oh you my silly baby I was kidding let's go those bubbles can't wait anymore to eat you up" he said blowing raspberry in her stomach she was a giggling mess.

He undressed her, while doing so he saw some scars on her back and stomach. He traces it with his finger, she was still giggling because it's ticklish the way he's tracing his finger "amm.... baby how did you get these scars" hearing that she tenses and silently tears came down rolling on her cheeks.

"Hey baby please don't cry you don't have to answer now take your time okay but is it the same person that cause this bruise on your forehead" he asked by placing his lips there kissing her forehead lovingly.

She sigh and was shocked he still remembered her bruised forehead. She thought he would let it go after her stupid made up lies. She didn't reply him so he just sighed and asked her whether she could bath herself or no she shook her head no. He smiled at that because he wanted to cherish every moment he spends with her. After bathing her he put on her clothes and they went downstairs stairs.

"Hey Mrs Williams look who I bring to see you" Cecilia was in the kitchen when they came down, on hearing that she squealed making Mia to bury her face in Alex chest fisting onto his shirt.

"You're scaring her Mrs Williams" he said

"Oh my am sorry dear I didn't mean to scare you am so excited to see you awaky come dinners ready and I made cookies for you too" she said making Mia turn to look at her

Waving at Cecilia, Mia said "hi Mrs Williams" nuzzling her face in Alex neck she was shy.

Alex chuckled at her "okay baby let's feed that your tummy with some yummies okay" she nods and let out a yawn starts closing her eyes.

"No princess you can sleep after dinner but not now okay I promise" he said shaking her a little bit.

After having dinner even though Alex tried to make Mia to eat more but she said she was full. He was satisfied with her eating habit for him she's kinda underweight because she looks smaller that her age. He decided to call his family doctor to come and check her up.

Cecilia brought some cookies for both of them wishing them a goodnight and left.

"Baby, baby girl look what Mrs Williams brought for us" she started to fall asleep when they came back to the room.

Her eyes lid up she crawled towards him, he placed her on his lap and cuddle her. "Yummy cookies for my beautiful baby" he said bringing up a cookie to her mouth she took a bite and moan.

He chuckled"yummy right" she nods, she eat about 3 of them he make her drink some warm milk.

He ate the remaining cookies and milk "baby let's sleep okay because tomorrow is going to be a long day for us we're gonna have so much fun" he said she just nod and let out a yawn placing her head on him chest cuddling him falling asleep.

He kissed her forehead lingering his lips there she smiled "goodnight dada" he heard her said.

"Goodnight dada's princess" God he have been waiting to hear that maybe because she felt safe with him that's why she called him that in her sleep either way he's happy she called him that.

"I love you baby girl more than you can imagine" he said caressing her cheeks he kissed it and cuddle her more and fall into a slumber having his princess close to his heart.

Hey guys hope you like this chapter.

Please comment, share and vote if you're loving this story.

Thank you

CHAPTER 5

Alex pov:

"Baby"I said shaking her a little she hummed."Hey sunshine it's time to wake up" she open her eyes, she smiled when she saw me."Good morning Mr. Alex" she said, I was a little disappointed because I thought she's going to call me dada as she said yesterday."Morning princess, how dis you sleep"I asked her."Good" she said smiling

"So today we're going to have lots of fun, we're going to the park, ice cream parlour and the mall" I said her eyes sparkled when I mentioned the ice cream parlour.

"Let's fresh you up and also make you eat some yummy breakfast made by Mrs Williams" i said tickling her, she giggles

"Okay" she said as she ran into the washroom with me chasing behind her.

After getting dressed we went downstairs and met Mrs Williams setting up the table for us we greeted each other and eat our breakfast.

"Princess you haven't even eat half of your waffle" i said because she push her plate aside saying that she's full.

I sigh"Mia you have to eat more please, 2 more bites for me" I said bringing a piece of waffle to her lips.

She ate it silently" umm am full Mr Alex thank you" she said.

"Okay have some orange juice" offering her the juice, she shook her head

" I don't wanna" she said.

" Just a little bit you don't have to drink it all just half of it pls baby" I said making a sad face.

"Okay, only half" she said taking the cup and sipping it I smile at her.

After having our breakfast, I make her put on her tiny sneakers she looked adorable. Putting my hand out for her to hold, we went into the parking lot to the car. I put her on the car seat and drive off to the mall.

After some few minutes we arrive at the mall. I unbuckled her from the car seat and out of the car.

" Princess we are going into the mall there are a lot of people here, do you want me to pick you up or hold my hand" I asked her, she was fisting my trouser as she looks around hesitantly.

She looked up making grabby hands for me and I pick her up. I place her on my hip.

"Am ready" she said, putting her head on my shoulder.

"Let's go in then baby" i said entering the mall.

We went to the kids sections there are a lot of kids clothes. I gently put her down for her to choose whatever she wants.

" Sunshine choose whatever you want, anything okay" I said as she look up.

"Anything" she asked and I nod.

She hesitantly point on a little black hoodie and a pair of black shorts and move back to me clutching onto my trouser again.

" That's all" she said I looked at her my eyes wide. I was surprised I thought kids love to shop or even like colorful, bright and sparkling things.

But she just wanted a black hoodie and shorts.

"Are you sure" I asked and she nods.

I signed and started picking up some random clothes for her like dresses, hoodies, sweats, skirts, shirts and many more.

"Mr. Alex"she said, I hummed in response.

I saw her pointing at a bear stuffie."Do you want it" I asked her, she shook her head and I frowned at that.

"No it's expensive" she said and I chuckled internally oh baby you don't know how rich your dad is I said to myself.

"No babygirl I told you to choose anything you want. You see your dad here can afford anything in this mall so feel free and pick anything I mean anything you want" I told her.

"I just want that bear, want penny to have a friend also to keep her company so she won't be lonely when am not with her" she said. I cooed at how adorable she looks like now she's so precious.

" Okay you're taking the bear and some more stuffies okay baby" I said and she nods.

After shopping we went to the ice cream parlour for some ice cream.

" Hello, good day what do you want to order" says the girl at the counter.

" Vanilla ice cream and chocolate chip topping and..." I look down at the little girl beside me.

" Princess what do you wanna have" I ask her.

" Chocolate chip ice cream and sprinkles" she chirped out.

" Okay" says the girl.

After getting our ice cream we went to the park and eat it there. Mia went to play with the other kids her age.

While I was on the phone, she came running up to me looking tired.

" Is my baby tired" I asked placing her on my lap, she nods yawning trying to keep her eyes open while failing miserably.

I took her back to the car and put the sleeping girl in her car seat and drive back home.

She was still sleeping when we arrived I just took her to our room place her on the bed so she could sleep comfortably.

Seriously she weightslike nothing, I let her sleep for two hours and woke her up to have her dinner.

While having dinner I saw how she was picking on her her food.

"Baby" she looked up.

" Why are you picking on your food" I ask her.

" Am not hungry" she answered.

"But baby you have to eat, it's for your own good don't you wanna be healthy and grow" I asked her, she shook her head.

" No I wanna be healthy and grow Alex" she said

" Okay the you have to eat more " I said and she started to eat her dinner even though it wasn't as I wanted her to but she tried.

"I am full" I heard her said.

"Then it's bed time right" she nods yawning

Taking her to the bedroom, she changed into her pjs after brushing her teeth and was ready for bed.

"Princess let's sleep" I said cuddling her more she hummed and close her eyes.

She has to start eating more, her health it's so important to me she has to be healthy. She's so skinny and weights like a feather, I have to take her to the doctor tomorrow.

I sigh "goodnight my love" I said kissing her temple making her snuggle into me I smiled and slept off.

Hope you like this chapter

And don't forget to comment, share and vote if you're like it.

Thank you

CHAPTER 6

Waking up doing their morning routine. They went downstairs to have their breakfast specially made by Mrs Williams.

"Princess today am taking you to a friend of mine, he's a doctor okay I don't want you to get scared because am going to be there with you the whole time" Alex said

She looked at him with wide eyes shaking her head as no" the hospital" she asked him

He nods " yes baby the hospital am taking you there for a regular check up okay" he said looking at her

"Okay Mr. A..a..Alex" she said stuttering.

He saw how terrified she looked and how she was trembling as he mentioned the hospital. His heart clenched whenever she calls him Mr Alex he yearns for her to call him daddy or even papa but since the day she called him dada when she was falling into a slumber she didn't ca him that again. He's always waiting and looking forward to when she's going to call him daddy not by him name.

" Princess no need to be scared he's my friend more like a brother. You remember my friend James right so he's his little brother his name is Andrew but known as Dr. Smith." He said.

"Am ready to go to the hospital" she said

"Okay baby go get your coat, we're going to meet your uncle James there at the hospital he's going with us for your check up" he said and she nods

she ran upstairs and grab her coat and came down running again.

"Mia princess stop running on the stairs I don't want you to get hurt okay baby" he told her when she came back running again.

"Okay Mr Alex I won't do it again" she said

"Promise" he asked her

"I pinkie promise pa... Mr Alex" she said

"Okay let's get going your uncle is already at the hospital waiting for us. We don't wanna keep him waiting do we" he asked her playfully.

She shook her head"no we don't" she said smiling.

They bid Mrs Williams bye and drove off to the hospital.On reaching there they saw James leaning against his car busy texting on his phone.

" Hey man, how have you been doing" Alex asked James approaching him.

" I'm good buddy and you" James asked him

" Same J" Alex answered

" Hey gorgeous, you remember me right your favorite uncle J" James said to Mia.

" Yes uncle J " she said

Alex clap his hands saying" okay let's go in and do this as soon as possible. I want to spend some quality time with my baby" he said winking at her.

Mia blush " okay" she said.

Entering the hospital they want straight to Dr. Smith's office as they already have an appointment with him and won't have to wait.

"Hi baby bro, how's work" James asked his little brother while entering his office.

Dr. Smith groan saying" don't you know what is called privacy, can't you just knock before barging into my office J" he said to James.

"Nope baby bro" James said popping the 'p' trying to find a seat.

"Don't mind him Andy you know how you brother is" Alex said

" I know Alex it's just whatever" Dr Smith said.

"Well hello there cutie pie" Dr. Smith said looking at Mia

Mia blushed hiding her face in Alex neck. He chuckled at her" Mia won't you say hi to Dr Smith" Alex said.

"Hello doctor" she said looking at Dr Smith.

" Aww she's so cute" he said.

"Baby bro can you please start" James said like he's annoyed.

" Can you please stop calling me baby bro am 24 for God's sake" Dr Smith said.

"And why would I do that baby bro" James asked him smirking.

"Andy let's just start with the check up, pretend that he's not here okay" Alex said.

" Okay lay her down there" he said pointing at a bed.

Mia clutch onto Alex shirt trying not to lay down on the bed shaking her head no.

Alex cooed saying" hey, hey baby everything's going to be okay, daddy's right here nothing's going to happen to you just trust me" he said

" Okay, stay here" she said laying down holding his hand.

"So let's get started" Dr Smith said.

He did all the regular checking he has to do and he sigh saying"Alex can you please come with me I want to talk to you outside please" he said

Hearing that Mia tighten her hold fearing that's he's gonna leave her there.

Sensing that Alex quickly said" hey baby calm down am not going anywhere and just gonna step out for a bit am come back for you okay" she nods.

"Okay" he smiled"thanks baby" he said.

Stepping out with Dr Smith he said" what is it that you don't want to say it in front of her" Alex asked him

Dr Smith sigh" she's malnutrished, she's too small for her own age and also she need some shots it's some vitamins that her body needs and it's urgent to give her those shots" he said to Alex.

Alex knew what he said was true but about the shots he doesn't know how she's gonna take those as she's so terrified at the idea of coming to the hospital.

" I know, so the shots how many are you talking about" he asked him.

" Three to be exact she needs it" Dr Smith said.

"Okay let's get it done with" Alex said going back to the office.

"Everything okay" James asked, Alex told him everything because Dr Smith went to get the shots. James looked at the small girl laying on the hospital bed feeling sad.

"Am back and it's time" Dr Smith said entering the office.

Alex went to Mia trying to distract her as Andrew start arranging the shots.

" Baby do you want to grab some ice cream after all this" he said distracting her as he saw Dr Smith heading towards her with the shots.

She beamed"yes I live ice cream" she said.

" Then we are getting it what about candy floss or even Cookie" he asked her as he saw the first shot in his hands.

Alex hold Mia's hand looking at Andrew as he start to give her the first shot.

" Yes candy floss and cook..." She screamed as she felt the need on her body.

She started shaking her head pleading Alex to take it out.

" Shh baby it's alright, princess you need the shots it's for your own good please baby stop crying just two more okay" he cooed saying that to her

Her eyes widened as she heard him say that there's more.

" No...n..no please I be good gwirl no more shots please Mr Alex tell him to stwop" she said sobbing.

Alex felt bad he can't see her cry like that, it's breaking his heart.

" Princess shh it will soon be over you are my brave girl right" he said.

She kept on screaming pleading them to stop she screamed again feeling the second shot

She said sobbing looking at James make grabby hands towards him" uncle J plwease tell them to stop"

He look at her feeling bad that he can't do anything about it because she needs them.

" P...pa..papa I be good girl no shots take it out" she said looking at Alex pleading him with her eyes.

Alex was ecstatic as she called him papa but couldn't show it at that moment because she needs him now to make her calm down.

" Shh baby calm down, no more tears I don't want you to fall sick from crying please" he said

"P..pa" she said hiccuping clutching onto his shirt.

She screamed at the last shot sobbing onto him again.

Rubbing her back saying sweet things in her ear trying to calm her down.

"It's over princess" he said cooing into her ears.

" Papa, p..papa, pa..." He heard her said as her hold loosened from him his shirt.

He holds her lifeless body as she becomes unconscious." Baby" he says shaking her.

He turned to Dr Smith who's trying to check her.

" She faint because she was scared she will be up in a couple of hours don't stress yourself she's fine" he said to Alex

Alex just nod and kept on staring at her stained face with dry tears and red nose from all the crying.

"Come and have a seat man, you heard him she's fine okay" James said.

Alex went and had a seat next to James but his gaze never leave his princess.

After a couple of hours Mia woke up. She saw that she was still in the hospital but Alex wasn't there.She saw Andrew going through some files. She sniffles thinking about Alex which caught Andrew's attention he quickly stood up and come towards her. She started crying calling her papa thinking Andrew is going to give her more shots.

" Shit, cutie your papa just step out to get something for you to eat when you get up he's coming back now" he said as he saw she's starting to have a panic attack.

" I want p...pa..papa" she said sobbing.

" I know he's coming back now okay please stop crying" he said.

Alex and James just entered the office and saw the scene upon them .

" Princess" he said walking towards her as he engulfed her into a hug.

" Pa...pa" she said hiccuping..

" Shh don't say anything, calm down Papa's here okay" he said kissing her head.

She kept on sniffling and nuzzling her face in the crook of his neck and she finally fall asleep as she exhausted herself with all the crying.

Alex saw that she's sleeping so he gently took her to his car not before thanking Dr Smith and also his friend James and bid them goodbye.

Alex went to the ice cream parlour and bought her the ice cream as he promised and went back home.

He carefully took her out of the car and went to their room. She starts to stir as he was about to lay her down on the bed.

" Papa" she mumbles in her sleep clutching onto him

" Shh baby am here just go back to sleep" he said she snuggles more as he lay down with her in his arms.

He place her on his chest stroking her hair placing small kisses time to time on her head.

He smiled as she snuggles more into him. He hugged her saying" sweet dreams princess papa loves you" he said kissing her cheeks. As he joins her in her little nap.

Alex felt like his the luckiest man on Earth because he was so ecstatic that his baby girl called him papa for the first time. He loves her so much like she's his own biological daughter. He can't wait just to spoil her and give her all what her hear desires. He also can't wait for his parents are siblings to meet her because he knows they are so gonna love her and spoil her as he planned to do.

Hello guys, well she called him papa for the first time yayy!!

What do you think about their relationship?

Hope you like this chapter and don't forget to vote.

Thank you

CHAPTER 7

"ALEXANDER DELUCA" he heard his mother's voice.

Shit he mumbled under his breath as he looks at his little bundle of joy who is cuddled up on his chest her face in his neck, hearing her soft snore she looks like an angel right now his little angel he thought.

"ALEXANDER GET YOUR BUTT DOWN HERE BEFORE I COME UP THERE AND GET YOU DOWN BY MYSELF" his mother shout again.

Oh my goodness why did I even give here a key to my house. God save me from her wrath.

"XANDER" oh no not this nickname, he knows that she only calls him Xander when she's pissed.

The worst part is that she knows that he was looking for a baby girl to adopt, but he haven't tell her that he adopted his little sunshine here.

"Princess daddy's gonna be right back" he says to her as he move her to lay her down properly on the bed, kissing her forehead.

She smiled like she heard what he was saying in her sleep, snuggling more under the covers she let out a soft sigh.

Alex went downstairs in a hurry when he saw his mother, father and siblings in his living room with wide eyes.

"Umm h-hey mom" he says stuttering.

"Xander I heard that you didn't go to the company for three whole day, if I may ask why" she said glaring at him.

Before he could answer her she cut him off by saying" and why do I have to hear from James that you have adopted a girl and I don't know the fact that I have a granddaughter now" she asked him again.

"M-mom I.. I" he says stuttering and scratching the back of his neck nervously.

"Mom I...I what" she asked him

He looked at his dad for help who looked away from him, while his siblings are trying not to burst out laughing. Traitors he mumbles under his breath.

"Am listening Xander" now she's pissed.

" Mom I haven't gone to the company because I was trying to make Mia to feel at home. I can't just go back to work after adopting her, she has to feel safe around me to warm up to me, to know things about her, what she likes and what not" he says looking at her with pleading eyes not to over react.

"Oh Mia's her name" she said like she's tasting how the name sounds on her tongue.

" Yes her name is Mia mom, and please stop with the glaring you're freaking me out" he says at that time his siblings couldn't hold it anymore as they burst out laughing.

"Ok but you have to make it up to me, because I thought something happened to you that's why you didn't go to work please don't scare me like that again baby" she says smile walking up to him to give him a hug and he nods.

Well ladies and gentlemen I present to you my overdramatic mother Emilia DeLuca, my father Gabriel DeLuca, and my two annoying siblings Aiden and Alisha DeLuca.

"So son how have you been doing and now you're a dad congratulations son am so proud of you" his dad said.

" Thanks dad" Alex said smiling.

"Yoo bro where's my niece I want to meet her, I have tons of things to do with her" Aiden says clapping his hands while Alex just roll his eyes.

" Yeah I can't see her anywhere or are you hiding her" Alisha said.

"N-n..." Before Alex could answer Aiden cuts him off

" Aww bro being possessive are we, you just kept her in here with you for three days wow" Aiden said with a smirk

" Well am gonna go make breakfast for you guys and especially my granddaughter" he's mother says heading to the kitchen.

" I will help you honey" his dad said following right behind her.

" So...." Alisha said.

"So what" Alex asked annoyed.

" Are you going to take us to meet her or what are we going to stand here possessive dad" Aiden said smirking looking at Alex reaction.

" She's sleeping we had a long day yesterday so yeah she's tired" Alex said irritatedly.

"It's 10 in the morning Alex you have to wake her up now or else she's going to be cranky all day" Alisha said sitting down on a couch in the living room.

" Okay I guess she has to wake up and eat some for because we slept off and skipped dinner" Alex said heading upstairs.

" Okay we will be waiting for you guys and don't be long or else you will see us barging into your room dear brother" Alisha says.

Alex sighed and shook his head and continue walking heading towards his room. On opening the door he saw Mia was stirring and starting to open her eyes. Her hand where searching for something but seems not to find it because she's half asleep. While trying to open her eyes Alex quickly walks up to her scooping her in his arms rocking her gently.

" Papa" she says caressing his cheeks to feel that he's right there.

" Yes princess it's me, how was your night" he asked her.

"Good papa" she says snuggling into his chest placing her face in his neck.

"Hey baby don't go back to sleep, there are some people downstairs who are here meet you" he said and she clutches his as he mentioned about her meeting new people she whispered.

She push face more into his neck still whimpering. "Baby if you don't want to meet them it's okay I can tell them you aren't ready to see them now okay". He said assuring her that there's no need for her to force herself to do what she doesn't wanna do.

"Who are they" she whispered quietly.

" It's my parents and siblings" he answered her.

"Huh" she looked at him tilting her head.

" Princess I mean my mom and dad, and also my brother and sister they are twins" he said.

" I have a grandma and grandpa" she asked smiling.

" Yes baby and also an aunt and uncle like your uncle J" he said stroking her hair.

" Okay I wanna meet them" she beamed her eyes sparkling with excitement.

She always wanted a grandma and grandpa. In the orphanage some of the kids used to talk about their grandparents but she never had one but now that she has she's going to have so much fun with them. She also have an aunt and two uncles she's happy.

"Okay sunshine like freshen you up and go downstairs to meet them" he said putting her down.

"Papa I hungry" she said looking at him.

" Okay baby let's be quick because grandma is making breakfast today" he said today is Saturday Mrs Williams went to visit her family she does that every weekend.

" Papa then we should hurry up" she said.

He was happy that now she's not hesitating to do things around him. She's warming up to him and he actually like it because they're going somewhere. He only wants her to be happy and feel safe around him.

"As you wish baby" he said entering the washroom.

After doing all the necessary morning routine the went downstairs to meet his family. She hide her face in his neck because she's feeling she at the moment.

" OMG Alex you didn't tell me that she's this cute" his mother squealed as she saw them coming down the stairs.

"Mom please keep it down you don't want to scare her do you" he said.

" Ohh hush am just excited to meet my pretty granddaughter" she said walking towards them, trying to pull Mia into her arms for a hug.

Mia clutches her Papa's shirts as she saw what she's trying to do.

"Hey princess you don't have to be scared they aren't going to hurt you, they just want to be your friends and know you okay" he said cooing.

" Okay papa" she mumbles.

Emilia awed at how cute she looks right now"can I hug you cutie pie" she asked Mia.

Mia looked at papa as he nods reassuring her that it's okay.

" Otay grandma" she said.

Her grandma hugs her" aww you're so precious to us baby" she says still hugging her.

" Okay mum it's now our time to meet our niece right Aiden" Alisha whined as she says.

" Yup so mom give her to me I wanna hold her too" Aiden says.

"Baby that is grandpa Gabriel, uncle Aiden, aunt Alisha and well grandma Emilia who's holding you now" Alex said.

" Hey, nice to meet you all" she said shyly.

The twins hugged her telling her all the fun things that they're are gonna do together.

" Grandpa" Mia says as she tug on her grandpa's pants.

" Yes munchkin" he answered.

" You're pretty" she said.

He chuckled at her adorableness" it's handsome pumpkin not pretty, am a man pretty is for ladies" he said.

" Oh, then you're handsome grandpa" she says smiling.

He bend a little to her eyes level" why thank you but you're gorgeous pumpkin" he says as he take into his arms.

" Okay let's go eat some breakfast" grandma says clapping her hands.

" Ahh thank God am starving" Aiden says rubbing his stomach.

His twin rolled her eyes saying" when aren't you hungry you foodie" walking towards the dinning room.

Everyone sit in their respectable seats as Emilia serve every one. They start eating Mia on Alex lap feeding her.

"Okay who's up for some fun" Aiden ask after having breakfast.

Alex groaned" not me am tired and so is my baby" he says nuzzling his nose in her neck. Which made her giggles as it tickles her.

" But I wanna play papa" she said.

"Okay then you should go" setting her down on her feet she ran to her uncle, who guide her outside to the garden to play with them.

"Alexander am so proud of you and happy for you son" his dad said smiling looking outside the window watching his kids playing with his granddaughter.

" Thank you dad it really means a lot, I appreciate it" he said to his father.

"Baby take good care of her okay she's an angel" his mother said.

" I will mom I promise" he said smiling.

That's how the spend the day talking, having fun, watching movies and a lot more.

Alex kept on smiling because as he knows his family will accept her and will also cherish her. He saw how happy she looks with his family hearing her giggles like music in his ears. He's so glad that she warmed up to his family not caging herself but was carefree with them. She saw her smile and happy that all he wanted from her because she felt safe around them and she's being herself. He loves her so much and feels like the luckiest man on Earth for having such an angel as his daughter.

Hey guys hope you like this chapter.

So she met his family, how do you think of them?

Don't forget to share, comment and share.

Thanks for reading

CHAPTER 8

Two weeks has passed like a blink of an eye. Alex made sure that Mia was comfortable with everyone that's around her she spends time with his parents and siblings during those two weeks. They went to the zoo, amusement park, cinema and so many places.

They had a lot of fun the twins took her to the mall and spoiled her rotten because they bought her alot of things like new stuffies even though she insisted that she has some but didn't listen to her, some dresses, shoes and many more. When they came back from the mall Alex eyes went wide as if they went and bought all the things in the mall.

Alex started to talk on how they are spoiling her too much, which the twins shush him say that she's their niece who are they going to spoil if not her.

Today is Monday meaning that Alex has to go back to work because he's behind schedule. He doesn't know how to approach his daughter who is sleeping peacefully on his bed right now.

"Baby" he whispered in her ear shaking her gently.

"Mmhm" she groan in her sleep.

" Princess it's time to wake up" he said caressing her cheeks.

" Papa" she mumbles while trying to open her eyes.

" Yes princess, hope you slept well" he said.

"Mmhm, morning papa" she said.

" Princess let's freshen you up okay" he said scooping her in his arms.

After doing their morning routine they went downstairs for breakfast, where they found Mrs Williams in the kitchen.

" Good morning lovelies" she said.

"Good morning to you Mrs Williams, how was your night" Alex said.

" It was good" she answered.

"Mowning Mrs Williams" Mia said.

" Morning to you too munchkin" she cooed.

"Papa I hungry" Mia said as she snuggles into him

"Okay baby what does my princess wanna eat for breakfast" he asked.

" Fwuits" she said.

"You mean fruits baby"he asked her.

She nods"yes papa fwuits" she said whining.

He chuckled" okay then fruit it is for my beautiful princess Mia here" he said walking towards the fridge the get some fruits for her.

" Alex you should sit at the dinning table I will just bring the fruits for her while you start eating your own breakfast" Mrs Williams said.

"No thanks Mrs Williams you have done more than enough, just go and have some I will handle this okay" he said.

" Okay then see ya in a bit, but are you going to the company today" she asked him.

He sighs" yes am going I have a lot of things to cover even though James was helping me with the company in my absence I have some things to check out which he can't" he said.

"Okay that good, what about Mia are you going with her or she's staying at him with me" she said.

" No am not going with she's not familiar with those kind of places, and am gonna be busy with work, I don't wanna make her feel neglected there so she's staying at home" he said.

" Okay good luck with convincing her as I know how she's so attached to you" she says chuckling as she walks away.

He knows that she's attached to him, she's always with him snuggling into him or cuddling with her papa.

He cut the fruits into small size suitable for her to eat it with ease.

" Baby where are you" he called when he didn't see her at the dinning table.

" Am here papa" she said her voice coming from the living.

" Okay baby am coming, stay where you are don't move okay daddy's princess" he said.

"Otay papa" she answered.

He took his breakfast, her bowl of fruits, a sippy cup filled with apple juice which is her favorite, and a cup of coffee for himself and went to the living. He saw her sitting on her on the carpet watching what seems like a cartoon she was so engrossed into that she didn't notice him.

"Sunshine" he said.

She got startled when she heard his voice" my fwuits papa" she said.

" Here you go and eat up as much as you can okay baby" he said giving her the bowl.

He took his own breakfast and start to eat it while sipping his coffee. When he was done he noticed she only ate half of it pushing the bowl towards him.

She mumbles" I full papa" she said.

" Aww baby can you more for dinner just two more bites please" he said making a sad face.

" Okay papa only two" she said.

After having the two bites he gave her the sippy cup which she took gladly and drink up all of the juice handling it back to her daddy.

He smiles at her " baby am gonna go upstairs to freshen up okay just stay here and enjoy what you're watching" he said kissing her forehead.

He took the dishes into the kitchen and went upstairs to freshen up.

He came back wearing a black suit ready to go to work. While Mia was trying to keep her eyes open as she was watching a movie now.

" My angel" he says in her ears as he scoops her in his arms kissing her temple.

She looked up at him and saw the suit that he's wearing now" papa where are you going" she asked as her lips starts quivering tears filling her eyes.

" Shh baby girl am not going anywhere far am going to come back before you know it" he says.

" N..no papa don't leave I be good girl pwease papa" she said clutching his suit sobbing.

" Baby you're always my good girl, shh am going to work princess I promise I will be back soon. I wish I could take you with me but am going to be so busy at the company" he said cooing into her ears while stroking her hair.

"No papa take me with you pwease" she says as her body starts to shake still sobbing.

He panicked" hey, hey baby please calm down follow my breathing please baby" he says looking at her

" Come on angel breath in and breath out" he said he kept doing that as she starts to calm down.

" Papa, papa, papa" she kept mumbling.

" I know baby, I know but please you have to understand I won't be long please can you be a big girl for daddy it will only take me a couple of hours" he said.

She shook her head no clutching his suit mumbling" stay with papa" he sighs.

" Baby am not leaving you alone you have Mrs Williams here with you, you guys are going to have lots of fun" she said trying to reason with her.

" Mia stay with papa only" she said quietly placing her head on his shoulder.

" Okay baby let's do this while daddy is at work why don't you make some brownies with Mrs Williams it's my favorite and I would be so happy if it was made by my little chef here after coming back all exhausted from work. Please baby can you do the for me" he said tickling her a little.

She said giggling " okay papa I be big girl for you and make brownies with Mrs Williams" he smiled looking at her.

"Okay baby thanks I can't wait to taste them because it's gonna be made by your magical hands" he said pecking her little nose.

She beamed"papa me have magical hands" she asked tilting her head.

" Yes my angel has magical hands" he said kissing her palms making his lips lingering for some seconds.

" Wow" she said clapping her hands.

He chuckles at her " okay baby I have to get going now" he said.

" Look at my hands Mrs Williams papa said I have magical hands and we are going to make his favorite bwonies for him" she said showing her hands to Mrs Williams who just walked into the living room.

" Wow that's really cool you're so lucky daddy's princess" Mrs Williams said.

" I know" Mia chirped.

" Baby come give papa a goodbye hug and kiss" he kneels opening his arm wide for her to come.

She ran towards him, she kissed his cheek and hugged him saying" okay go now and come back soon me and Mrs Williams will be making your bwonies bye" she said pushing him towards the front door.

" Wow baby I didn't know you want me gone this easily" he said pouting.

She huffs " oh papa if you keep standing here you can't go to the office then we won't start making the bwonies for you now go" she said pushing him further.

He bend down to her eye level kissing her temple says" bye princess be a good girl for Mrs Williams, see you in a couple of hours I love you" he said walking out of the house.

" I lub you too Papa" she said as she skipped towards Mrs Williams dragging her into the kitchen.

" Whoa sweetheart I see you are excited" she said to Mia.

" Yes am so happy and making bwonies for papa with my magical hand" she said.

Alex went straight to his company as he entered his employees started bowing their heads greeting him as he walk passed them without sparing them a glance.

Alexander DeLuca to his family he is the biggest softie, loving and a caring so, brother and a family only to his family. But to the business world he's a devil his face is always blank with no emotion, his employees thinking that he doesn't smile but little did they know he can do more than that with his family and especially with his beautiful angel. They think that way because he has an emotionless expression on his face always.

He went into his office as his PA brought him his coffee as always filling him with what he was scheduled for the day.

" Hey man how's it going" James says entering the office.

Alex sighs as he has been working for the last 6 hours non-stop" good I guess" he said.

"Ohh I can see that, how's my little niece doing" he said chuckling at Alex as he saw the files on his table.

" She doing great but she had a little tantrum as she doesn't want me to leave her but I convinced her to stay by tricking her to make brownies for me with Mrs Williams" he said smiling.

"Aww that's adorable I wish I was there to see the scene to watch how you will go all soft on her" James said.

"Whatever, am just trying to finish this and head home am tired man" Alex said.

" Well I will be going back now, I just came in to check up on you, you know how Melody is bye" James said walking out of the office.

"Bye and my regards to Melody" Alex said.

After another 2 hours he was done and was heading home. He was so exhausted but at the same time excited to see his princess.

On the other hand Mia and Mrs had made the brownies which were cooling down. Mia babbling to her about her stuffies and what not.

Mia was rambling on about her papa when he's coming back home. Because she cannot wait for him to come and taste the brownies she made with her magical hand.

Alex came back home around 8 in the night. He found his bundle of joy on their bed wearing one of his t-shirts playing with her stuffies seems like she's having a tea party with them. She was so engrossed in her party that she didn't feel his presence in the room.

He gently walk towards her and scooped in his arms which make her squeal in surprise" papaaaa" she said whining.

"Aww princess I missed you so much" he said nuzzling his face in her hair.

" Papa I missed you more" she said hugging him.

" No baby girl I missed you more" he said mimicking her.

" Papaaaa" she said.

"Babyyyyy" he said winking at her.

" Papa come let's go you have to taste the bwonies I made with my magical hands" she said showing her hands to him.

He kissed it" ohh then they are going to taste better than any brownies that I have ever tasted in my life because it was made by my beautiful princess magical hands" he said.

" Okay papa let's go" she said dragging him downstairs.

They went downstairs and ate something of the brownies and had some juice with it.

"Yummy" Mia said.

" Mmhm wow princess these are the best brownies that I have ever tasted in my life they're so delicious" he said taking the last bite of his brownies.

" Of course I was made by me" she says proudly.

" I know princess, now it's time for bed let's go" he said holding his hand out for her.

" Otay papa" she said holding his hand as they walk upstairs.

They went straight to bed as they entered the room.

" Goodnight papa, l lub you" she said kissing his jaw as that's where she could reach while laying on his chest.

" Night princess I love you more" he said pecking her forehead and went into a deep slumber as he was exhausted.

Hey guys done with this chapter.

Don't forget to vote, comment and share if you are liking this story.

Thanks for reading

CHAPTER 9

It's been two months seen Mia was adopted. Alex has been busy with work always leaving early in the morning and coming back last in the because of some pending work he had at the company. In his absence his employees were slacking off at work, so he had to make everything g back to the way it is. For him everything has to be perfect.

And Mia she has been spending time with his family and Mrs Williams for the past couple of weeks. But she's missing her papa who's always there for her but now he has been too busy to even play with her which makes her so sad.Even though Alex always never missed a chance to kiss or hug whenever she's sleeping or awake he always cuddles with her we he comes back late from work and founds her sleeping on their bed.

Alex have been really worried about their relationship now because he feels like he's neglecting her and he doesn't want her to feel like he abandoned her for him work. To Alex nothing matters to him more than Mia she's his priority.

Mia on the other her start to feel insecure thinking that her papa doesn't love her anymore, maybe because she's a bad girl and ugly like what Emily said to her. She thinks that he realizes that she's not good enough for him.

His parents and siblings noticed how he has been busy and have not been spending time with his daughter as he use to be. So his mother is going to knock some sense into him.

Alex was in his office, files scattered everywhere on his table, he's typing furiously on his computer he was so engrossed in whatever he was typing when the door of his office was slammed open. He groaned and look up to see who was it, thinking it was James who has been annoying him since morning but to his suprise it was his mother.

She was fuming, he can see the smoke coming out of her ears literally . Ohh this isn't going to be good.

" ALEXANDER ACE DELUCA" she said as she walks towards him.

Oh no with the middle name this time, this is bad, this is so bad, so so bad it won't end well (rest in peace Alex) he thought to himself.

He scratches the back of his neck saying" hey mom"

She slammed her hands on the table and said" don't you dare hey mom me. Alexander i have taught you better than this"

He furrowed his eyebrows" i don't get what you're saying, what did I do. Ohh did the twins said something stupid am gonna ki...." Before he could finish he was cut off by her saying.

" No Xander am gonna kill you before you even touch a strand of their hair" she said glaring at him as she continues to say.

" I have never expected something like this from you, if you know you're going to abandon her at home with some maids to take care of her why did you even adopt her. You son she doesn't deserve how you're treating her seriously I envy your relationship with her because the way you guys bond in short a period of time I didn't even have that kind of bond you have with you and your siblings" she said sighing.

His body stiff a little bit but relaxed " mom I love her so much why would you say that am abandoning her. That kid means a lot to me mom, she's my baby, my angel heck my world revolves around her" he said putting his hands through his hair.

" Son I know you love her but you have to create time for you guys to spend together. You know the first time she came she only trusted you, doesn't want to get separated from you. You're always together think about it are you like that now" she said glaring at him.

He sighs" I know we became a little distant ... " She raised her eyebrow " okay well I became distant because of work am sorry Mom" he said.

" Look am not pressuring to do something extravagant to make it up to her because I know my kids are kinda silly in doing stuffs like this" she said smiling at him.

He smiles back at her saying" I will mom I will make it up to all of you not only my baby girl"

" If you don't do that soon I may or may not make them to take her custody from you and give her to a more decent family who will love her as she deserves. She such an angel for anyone to refuse raising her when they get a chance" she says playfully, she knows what she said will trigger him and she hit some nerves.

She was cut off in her thoughts with a sound that she cringe at, well as she thought there stood Alex fuming shooting daggers into her as he stares at her. He walks towards her each step he tooks makes a cracking sound cause of the vase he threw which broke into million pieces.

" Like hell you would, no one I mean no one can take my princess away from me even if it's you or dad or even anybody who dares to think about taking my baby from me will face hell on Earth" he said trying to calm down as he thinks about their happy moments with his daughter.

" Hey Alex I didn't mean it like that am sorry son I was just teasing you" she said hugging him, she knows herself won't let anyone tell their little munchkin from them talkless of her doing that to her own son it will be so cruel of her.

He sighs hugging her" I know mom buh you know how hit some nerve" he said playfully glaring at her.

" Oh my heart" she said placing her hand on her heart making a painful expression her face like it hurts" buh you love me thou' " she said winking at him.

Drama queen he thought" yeah yeah whatever I love you beyond your imagination momma" he teases her.

" You know I came to your office straight from your house because of the situation I found Mia in that's why I was furious with you as I entered" she said looking at him.

When she mentioned Mia name that got his attention which eyes widened and he went in to panic mode " wh... what do you mean mom. Did something happened to my baby is she okay please tell me mom". He said trying to calm his breath.

" Hey calm down, breath in and breath out" he did as she says.

" Please momma" he said, she saw how vulnerable her son looks she knows how much he loves that girl.

She looked into his eye that turned bloody red, she doesn't know how he's gonna take this but she sighs saying" well I went to your house to check up on you guys, and I saw Cecilia holding on to Mia who's puking her guts out" she said and his body tenses against hers.

His baby wasn't feeling well and he's here working his ass off not knowing how his daughter is doing. No wonder her body feel a little warmer than usual yesterday.

She continues but this time hugging cause she doesn't know how he will react when he hears the last part. She remembered a time when Mia fell while she was running away from the twins and got a small scratch on her hand Alex flipped and banned her from running afraid of her getting hurt again.She doesn't want him to blaming himself for what she's going to say now cause she knows her son he's going to blame himself for not being a good father for their princess.

Her hold tighten against him saying" she looks a little pale, her temperature rises, she has been puking since yesterday morning whenever she eats food. She even fainted when I was asking Cecilia about her condition that's when I called the family doctor. He said it was nothing major just a slight food poising that cause her to throw up and how small she is for her own age so it hit her hard, but he gave her some shots that will help her rest for a couple of hours and prescribed some medicine for her to take which will also her with the puking. He suggested to give her liquid food for the next 3 days after that she can take solid food" she said.

" Cecilia wanted to tell you but you came back late in the night and left the next morning early so she couldn't tell you pls don't be mad as to why you weren't told about your daughters situation" she said

There was silence in the office" Alex, hey baby talk to momma okay am here for you" she said stroking his hair, he only tightened his hold against her.

She felt wetness on her bare shoulder" baby please talk to me and please don't cry it's not your fault" she said rubbing his s back trying to calm him down.

" Momma am such a bad father she deserves someone who will take care of her better than I do" he said sniffling.

" Alex don't you dare say that again you're a good father she really adores you and loves you so much" she said breaking the hug looking straight into his red eyes.

" But momma she must have hat..." He was cut off with her saying

" Shhh don't say that pls she loves you so very much no matter what, you know why I said that" she said and he shook his head.

" Before she fall asleep after the doctor gave her some shots, which I might say she did well, she said I shouldn't tell you about her being sick" she said

" No mom" he said.

She chuckles and said" she said no tell papa cause papa will worry about me and be sad I only want papa to be happy not sad "

He smiled at the thought that his daughter cared about his feeling but soon vanishes when he remembered she must be in so much pain.

" So I need you to calm down and take care of what's on your table and take a week off James will handle the company in your absence and go take care of your daughter" she said.

" No am going straight home to my daughter she needs me" he said picking up his phone.

" I know she does but she will be out for the next 3 hours just try to finish this quickly and go to her as soon as possible cause I want her to wake up with you by her side okay" she said

" Okay mom I will do as you say" he said walking back to his table.

" Alright then expect to see us all at your house tomorrow cause you know your dad and siblings won't be taking it lightly so am gonna leave guys together today but not tomorrow am gonna take care of my grandbaby so bye son and love you" she said heading towards the door.

" Thanks for everything momma love you more" he said opening a file.

Alex finished everything in one and a half hour and went straight home to his princess.

He found her sleeping soundly on their bed a wet towel on her forehead, she looks so pale and small my poor baby he thoughts.

He went into the washroom took a shower and change into some comfy clothes and walks towards the bed to see her shivering.

" My baby, am so sorry please forgive me Papa's sorry I will never leave you ever again" he said as he lay down on the bed scooping her in his arms and placing her on him, he hugs her like his life defend on her.

He kisses her forehead, rubbing her back and stroking her hair which she let out some sighs time to time.

" Princess I love you so very much" he said kissing her hair.

" Papa will make it up to you I promise pls just be better" he said nuzzling his face in her hair.

She stir in her sleep clutching onto his hoodie she said absentmindedly"papa" in her sleep.

He cooed at her" yeah princess am right here with you and not going anywhere you stoke with me " he said.

He kept on dropping kisses on her hair, forehead and anywhere his lips can reach on her.

He was holding her so tight to his body like someone's gonna snatch her away from him with that he went into a deep slumber with his baby in his arms knowing that she's there with and no one's taking her away from him, he sighs with content.

Hola readers am sorry for not updating soon enough for you guys.

So what do you think of this chapter, well to me I felt like crying it made me so emotional.

And what's your opinion on Alex in this chapter is he a good father or not?

Hope you like it and don't forget to vote, share and comment if you're loving this story.

Thanks for reading I really appreciate it

CHAPTER 10

S nuggling more into her dad's warm chest Mia started to stir in her sleep whimpering softly. She's all sweaty, her hair was everywhere in a mess, her shirt was wet from all the sweat. She was feeling cold but she's sweating and shivering at the same time, she clutches her Papa's hoodie putting her head in the crook of his neck needing skin to skin contact with him eagerly.

Alex hold her firmly into him he felt that she kept stirring in her sleep her keep rubbing her back because he knows she's in pain. He heard her whimpers that's when he opened his eyes and saw her all sweaty, shivering like she's freezing. He starts to panic seeing her in that condition, that when she put her head in the crook of his neck needing the skin to skin contact. He understood what she wanted when he tried to remove her head from there as she whined in her sleep absentmindedly.

"P...pa...pa" she mumbles as she starts to open her eyes which felt heavy for her.

" Shh baby Papa's right here" he cooed into her ears but his voice betrayed him it cracked a little seeing her condition.

" Papa n..no" she struggles to say something to him.

"Princess don't stress yourself okay am right here with you" he said.

She starts shaking her head saying" no leave me I be good girl" clutching his hoodie trying to put her head in the crook of his neck again.

" Hey baby am not leaving you okay, never ever leaving you. Am so sorry princess Papa's sorry it's all my fault if o haven't neglected you, you won't be suffering right now I should be the one suffering not you my precious" he said burying his face in her hair inhaling her lavender scent to calm his nerves.

With a shaky hand she touch his cheek wiping away his tears saying" no cry papa, see am okay" she forced a smile at him trying to make him feel better.

" Am still sorry sunshine, I will keep on apologizing to you and I will make it up to you. You will never feel abandoned or neglected again I will do my best to be the best father to you baby I pinky promise you" he said crossing his own pinky with her tiny one.

She saw how hers was so small in his she tried to giggle but it came out as a groan" papa" she said breathlessly hugging him like her life depends on him.

" Baby let's run you a warm bath yeah" he said trying to pick her up from his chest and lay her down on the bed in order to do so but she whimpers.

" No, no leave papa" she said sobbing into the crook of his neck and clutching onto to him.

" Hey baby am not leaving you am just going into the washroom to run you a warm bath so you will feel better and then we will eat some of Mrs Williams delicious foods and cuddle in bed with each other maybe watch some of your favorite movies or cartoons baby" he said rubbing her back trying to calm her down.

" No no leave Mia, Mia stay with papa" she said sniffling.

" But baby I won't be far from you it's just the washroom room and you will be on the bed" he said as he starts to lay her down on the bed.

Her hold tightens against him and her body starts to shake as she's in a full sob now hiccuping saying his name repeatedly.

He saw how her body is shaking he doesn't want her to be more sick as she is right now so he sighs as got out of bed with her clinging to him burying her face in the crook of his neck sniffling as she was all exhausted from all the crying she did. He runs her a warm bath and tries to remove her from him but she only tightens her hold.

He sighs"baby I need to bathe you please it will make you feel better" he cooed in her ear rubbing her back gently.

She nods saying" Otay papa, but u stay with Mia" looking at him with her red hopeful eyes.

" Am not going anywhere okay" he said kissing her head.

He removed her clothes and put hr inside the bathtub, he heard her sighing heavily and she enjoys the warm water.

He took her out as the water starts to get cold, put a fluffy towel on her and took her the bed and lay her there.

" Hey shh baby am just going into the closet to get you some warm clothes okay" he said as he saw her wide eyes and her lips starts to wobble she taught he was leaving her.

" Papa" she said making grabby hands at him sniffling.

He took her in his arms and walks towards the closet picked out some clothes for her and went back to bed to dress her. After dressing her he called Mrs Williams to bring them some soup because it's time for her to take her medication and she has to eat something at least.

" Hey there sweetie, how are you feeling now" Mrs Williams said as she placed the food down looking at Mia.

She snuggles into her dad more say a soft " otay" closing her eyes.

" May you recover soon okay" she said walking out of the room.

" Thank you Mrs Williams" Alex said before she head out.

He adjust her on his lap in order for her to eat properly" okay baby let's put this yummy chicken soup in to this your tummy" he said kissing her cheeks.

" Papa" she said looking at him.

" Yes baby" he said kissing her temple.

"Mia no hungry" she said.

" I know baby but you have to eat this food in order to take your medicine, can you do this for Papa it will make you feel better" he said with pleading eyes.

" Otay for papa" she said smiling she doesn't want to make him sad even though she doesn't feel like eating anything.

" Thank you baby" he said kissing her nose which made her smile.

After making her eat the soup he made her take the medicine with she didn't take well, which caused them to have a big fight but at the end forced her to take it saying it will make the pain go.

She's glaring at him now because he gave her a yucky medicine" meany papa" she said

" Aww is my baby am angry" he said.

" Yes I is angry y...you no love me that's why you gave me that bitter medicine" she said sniffling.

" No baby I love you with all my heart, you are my world and I gave it to you because it's for your own good. If you're angry with me for caring for you then it's okay keep being angry with me because I will do anything to make you feel better and healthy even if it will make you angry or hate me angel" he said walking into the washroom to take a shower.

He knows that what he said wasn't the right thing to say right now looking at her vulnerable state. Mia on the other hand starts to cry quietly because she thinks that she made him angry she's gonna make him hate her and will send her back to the orphanage.Her lips starts to quivers as she thought of the words her bullies told her that one day he will get tired of her and will send her back because she is ungrateful.

Alex came back into the room dressed in a t-shirt and sweatpants. He heard her whimpers and sniffles, he saw her shaking in the verge of having a panic attack he ran towards her taking her into his arms.

"Hey, hey baby calm down am here now Papa's going to making things all better hmm" he said rocking them both.

" Papa, papa, p..paa" she said sobbing clutching onto him.

" Shh am not leaving you okay baby try to follow my breathing okay baby" he said rubbing her back.

" I sowwy papa no I take Mia back" she said burying her face in his chest.

" Baby take you where, I don't get you mean the orphanage" he said hugging her.

She nods" yes" she said sniffling her body still shaking.

Hearing her his hold on her tightens clenching his jaw" shh baby stop crying you're my precious baby, I will never I mean never take you back there I promise you sunshine. I love you so much to even think of taking you back there" he said kissing her forehead.

" Baby you mean the world to me, I won't let anyone take you away from me talkless of me taking you back to that place that treated you badly" he said hugging her burying his face in her hair and kissing it.

" Baby are you listening to me" he said because her body stopped shaking and couldn't hear her sniffling.

He felt her body goes limp in his arms as he tries to see her face because she wasn't responding to him.At first he thought she was sleeping but after shaking her for a couple of times she didn't respond he kept on shaking her small body.

" Baby please" his voice cracking.

" Mrs Williams" he yelled for her to come.

She came in running after hearing her name being called" what's wrong ale..." She couldn't finish what she was about to say. " Oh dear" she said placing her hand on her mouth.

" Please call Dr Smith" he said sniffling hugging his princess.

" Okay dear" she said rushing downstairs to get her phone and call the doctor.

Alex kept hugging his baby in his arms crying for her not to leave him

" Baby papa is sorry please don't leave me, princess I can't leave without you please I love you so much" he said kissing her head.

" I called him, he's on his way" she said looking at him, she has never seen him in such a vulnerable state.

" She's going to be okay dear" she said to him.

" It's all my fault Mrs Williams I haven't been neglecting her this wouldn't have happened" he said crying hugging her.

" It's not your fault Alex" she said.

" No it's my f..." He started saying when James and Dr Smith barged into the room.

" Oh my God what happened to them" James asked.

" Pls check what's wrong with her" he said looking at Dr Smith.

He layed her down on the bed and the doctor starts checking her" what happened" he asked Alex.

As Alex told him what happened, the doctor sighs and said" it's nothing serious something triggered her that's why she got scared and fainted. She will be fine and will wake up in the morning" he said to Alex.

" But I didn't do or said anything that will trigger her. I was shocked when she was begging me not to take her back I love my baby so freaking much to even think of someone taking her away from me talkless of me being the one sending her away" Alex said wiping his tears looking at his angel who's now sleeping.

" I know man but fix this when she wakes up and don't get scared when he has a fever during the night because am sure she may have one just do the bases which I have shown you when James was ones having one" Dr Smith said leaving the room telling them to take care.

" Am gonna come back tomorrow to check up on you guys okay take care bud" James said as he heads out of the room too.

" Am gonna go make something for you to eat dear" Mrs Williams said.

" No am good thanks though" he said forcing a smile.

" Okay dear but remember it's not your fault and this cutie pie adores and loves you so much she sees you as her role model. Don't be hard on yourself okay and goodnight" she said as she leaves the room.

" I will try not to thanks" he said.

Looking at his princess he lays beside her and moved her close to him hugging her like his life depends on her.

" Am really sorry princess Papa's loves you so much and I will make everything better you won't have to be scared anymore thinking you will lose me baby am the one scared of losing you" he said caressing her cheeks.

She whimpers in her sleep hearing that his heart clenched hearing her whimpering, he hugs her tightly burying his face in the crook of her neck saying how much he loves her and how sorry he is.

Mia fainted because she was scared that he's going to take her back to the orphanage that now he's tired of her being with him. Unfortunately she was wrong because Alexander love her to dead and wants nothing but what's best for her and her happiness means a lot to him.

He always wants to see her happy and bubbly, he loves her so much that he can do anything for her in order to make her happy.

Hello guys hope you like this chapter.

Don't forget to vote, comment and share if you're like this story.

Any thoughts from anyone?

Thank you for reading.

CHAPTER 11

I t was around 7am in the morning, Mia started to stir in her sleep as she felt soft kisses all over her face. She buried her face in the crook of his neck trying to sleep more as she was so exhausted from yesterday's event.

Alex chuckled at her cuteness" hey baby, good morning" he said kissing her temple.

"Mmph" she hummed hugging him.

" Princess you have to wake up now okay, you can take a nap later I know you are exhausted please" he said rubbing her back.

She slowly opened her eyes looking at him she smiled but as soon as she remembered what happened yesterday her eyes becomes glossy.

" Good mowning pa..." She said her voice cracked at the end.

" Hey cupcake shh what's wrong, are you in pain please talk to me baby" he starts to panic as he saw tears running down her cheeks.

She shook her head" no am feeling much better than yesterday" she said with a sad smile.

"Then what's wrong, did I do something to upset you or anything that you didn't like" he said his voice becoming low.

"No pa... Mr Alex you didn't do anything" she said smiling at him.

His heart clenched hearing her call him by his name. Did he messed up so bad that triggered her to go back to the way they were. He couldn't believe his ears hearing her calling him Mr Alex. He's going to fix this he can loose his baby girl because of his stupidity.

Mia thought calling his with Mr Alex will lessened what happened yesterday because to her he doesn't want her now maybe because he can see how useless she is. So she can't be selfish and be calling him her papa it's not right even though she loves calling him that.

She hops out of bed and went into the washroom and did her morning routine and went downstairs for breakfast as she was feeling much better but a little bit dizzy but she can manage.

" Good morning Mrs Williams" she said smiling at her.

" Morning sweetie" she replied back.

She saw Alex sitting down in one of the chair in the dinning room silently eating his breakfast.

" Here have some breakfast" she said placing a plate of chicken soup in front of her.

" Thank you" she said.

" Okay enjoy dearies" Mrs Williams said when she saw the tension that feels the air between the two.

She looks at Alex glaring at him which means 'fix what you did' and left the room.

Mia tried to feed herself but she kept on failing woefully because her hands shakes whenever she scoops some of the soup, she sighed and took the glass cup filled with orange juice carefully not to spill with shaky hand.

After drinking half of it she stood up and was ready to leave the dinning room, when she heard Alex clearing his throat.

Alex have been watching her every move since she came into the dinning room but kept quiet. When he saw her failing miserably when she tries to feed herself and drank half of the orange juice. She was ready to leave when he cleared his throat gaining her attend.

He chuckled internally when he saw he flustered face like she was caught stealing a cookie.

" Where do you think you are going baby" he asked her.

" I umm I " she mumbles.

He raised an eyebrow at her" yes"

" I am full papa oh sorry Mr Alex" she said.

" Really you haven't even touched the food princess" he said softly.

"It's so fwustwating (frustrating) papa" she whined.

Alex smiled at her cause she didn't realise she even called him papa.

" What's so frustrating baby" he ask.

" The meanie soup" she huffs crossing her arms.

" That meanie soup has to be inside you tummy miss Mia" he said playfully glaring at her.

" But papa I can't..." She started saying.

" Baby I will feed you" he said smiling.

" No Mr Alex you don't have to, you have done more than enough for me" she said smiling sadly at him.

He frowned at what she said " princess come here" he said.

She walks slowly towards him, when she was close enough he scoops her in his arms and place her on his lap.

He hugged her burying his face in her hair saying how sorry he is.

" Cupcake please forgive daddy am so sorry" he said still hugging her.

" It's okay Mr Alex I forgive you" she hugged him too.

" No no baby you didn't" he said shaking his head.

" I do forgive you" she said burying her face on his chest.

" Princess then why are you calling me Mr Alex instead of papa" he said and she freeze.

" I..I" she stuttered.

" You what baby" he asked.

" I thought you no love me anymore and you will be taking me back to the orphanage. So I don't wanna be selfish and have you all to myself that's why I started to call you Mr Alex. If I call you papa it will be hard for me. I don't know what to do without you papa I love please don't take me back I will be a good girl please" she said crying.

" Shh baby I love you more than you can imagine, am taking you back I will never do that ever. If someone tries to even take you away from me they will have to face hell on Earth princess. You mean the world to me I can't leave without you and hearing you calling me Mr Alex broke my heart which made me so so sad baby" he said rubbing her back trying to calm her down.

" No papa don't be sad, I don't want my papa to be sad I want him to be all all happy happy" she said giggling.

" Oh my sunshine how much I missed your giggles" he said kissing her all over her face.

" I love you Papa" she said kissing his cheek.

" I love you more baby girl" he said.

He fed her the chicken soup and took her upstairs to freshen up again since she made a mess while having her soup and gave her, her meds.

" Papa I wanna wear your shirt" she said.

" Okay anything for my princess" he said bowing which made her giggle.

" Papa" she said.

" Yes buttercup" Alex said as he walks out of the closet.

She smiled at him because she loves all the nicknames that he calls her with.

" Papa I love you and grandpa and grandma and uncle James and aunt Alisha and uncle Aiden and and..." She started rambling.

" Hey princess calm down okay we all love you too" he said.

" That's true pumpkin" a voice said which made them to look at the door.

" Hey Dad" Alex said.

" How are you doing my little munchkin" he asked Mia who ran towards him stumbling at every step she took because of the shirt yelling ' grandpa's.

"Am good grandpa" she said hugging his legs.

" Awwn someone missed me" he said taking her in his arms.

" So much where's grandma and the twins" she asked.

" They are downstairs waiting to see you" he said walking downstairs while Alex was following them closely behind.

" Hey mom" Alex said.

" Mia my baby" she said walking towards her husband.

" Grandma" she said giggling.

" Baby how are you doing today" she asked her.

" Am doing good grandma, Papa's taking good care of me" she said looking at Alex smiling at him.

" Aww that's great, I brought you all your favorite food" she said.

" Yummy thank you Grandma I love you" she kissed her cheeks.

" Aww baby I love you too" she said.

" Where's that shortie I can't see her anywhere" Aiden said pretending he can see her.

" Am right here uncle Aiden" she said standing in front of him.

" I can hear her beautiful tiny voice but can't see her and where" he said walking past her still pretending he didn't see her.

" Argh uncle Aiden can you see me now" she ran after jumping in front of him waving her hand.

" Ohh now I can see you, hey shortie" he said teasing her.

She huffed and ran towards her papa" Papa uncle Aiden is a meanie" she said panting.

" Hey baby don't run and jump too much, you just gotten better can you that for me" he said concerned.

" Okay papa for you" she said smiling and kissed his jaw.

" Thank you baby" he said kissing her forehead.

" Aiden stop teasing my baby she's not that short right honey" her grandma said.

" Yes grandma am tall just like my papa" Mia said.

" Well isn't this great you guys forgetting about me" Alisha said.

" Aunt Ali i love you" Mia said hugging her.

" Awwn cutie pie I love you too" Alisha said kissing her cheeks.

Alex roll his eyes at his family" seriously guys have you forgotten am part of this family too, mom even you too I wasn't expecting it from you or dad but this two argh whatever" he said.

" Am guys can you smell something" Aiden said teasingly.

" ahh I think I can" Alisha said.

" Hmm smells like jealousy" their mom said.

" Seriously son are you jealous of your own daughter getting all the attention from us" his dad asked him.

Alex huffs and said" no am not I can never be jealous of my princess cause she deserves all the love and attention she gets" kissing her palms.

" Papa is not jealous he loves me" Mia said hugging his legs.

" Of course princess papa loves you so very much" he said taking her into his arms burying his face in her hair inhaling her sweet lavender scent.

" Aww am gonna cry" his mom said fanning her face.

" Gosh you guys are so dramatic" Aiden stated rolling his eyes.

" Oh hush you idiot" Alisha said.

" Okay let's have some lunch" grandpa said.

They had their lunch and played some games. During the game Mia sat on her dad's lap and kept yawn now and then. Alex noticed her eyes were dropping slightly and started rocking them back and forth in a couple of minutes she was out like a light.

He took her to their room and place her on their bed and went downstairs to spend more time with his family as she get some rest.

" Am so proud of you son" his dad said.

" Yeah so so proud you baby boy" his mom said.

" Thank you momma" he said hugging her.

" Ohh momma's boy is back" Aiden teased.

" Shut up" Alex huffs.

" Seriously you guys should start a show cause you're so dramatic" Alisha said annoyed.

They kept on teasing each other and playing games with each other because it have been long for them that they spend time like this with each other which they really enjoyed.

After a couple of hours Alex woke up Mia in order to take her medication which she did well and did cause any tantrum.

She did leave her father's side when she woke up she was glued to him. She clung on to him like a koala cuddling him. Or playing with his hair, fingers and his shirt buttons.

" Papa" she said looking into his eyes.

" Yes baby" he said caressing her cheeks.

" I love you Papa" she said blushing and hide her face in the crook of his neck feeling shy.

" Aww baby I love you too" he chuckled kissing her hair.

That's how they spend the day with his family. After dinner his family went home and he had a movie night with his princess. She was out like a light in the middle of the first movie cuddling with her dad.

He looks at her sleeping form and smiled. He kissed her forehead and cuddles her more into him and continue to watch the movie which he watched like two more before he calls it a night.

He cuddles her closer to him saying how much he loves her and will protect from the world. And went into a deep slumber his face buried in her hair thinking of what he and his family had planned for her tomorrow.

Hello lovelies

Sorry for the late update, hope you are enjoying this story.

Don't forget to vote, comment and share.

Thank you for reading

CHAPTER 12

Mia woke up giggling as she felt the soft kisses all over her face with a smell of fresh cooked food. She opened her eyes and saw it was none other than her dad who's showering her with kisses.

"Good mowning papa" she said smiling.

"Morning princess, how did you sleep?" He asked.

" Good papa" she kissed his jaw giggling.

"Mhm great, so a brought your favorite food waffles with chocolate syrup, with a little bit of strawberries and your chocolate milkshake" he said looking at her while licking his lips.

" Yummy you made it for me papa" she asked tilting her head a bit.

" No grandma made it, they are all downstairs waiting for us to get ready" he said kissing her forehead.

She beamed when she heard that they were downstairs and was ready to go down until Alex hold her" papaaaaa" she whined.

" Baby you have to eat your breakfast first and you have to freshen up too then we can go down to meet them and also your suprise" he said winking at her as he said suprise cause he knows she loves surprises.

" Suprise papa" she said with a big smile on her face.

" Yes baby a surprise just for you" he said kissing her palms.

" Otay I will brush my teeth now" she said running into the washroom.

" Be careful princess no running" he said and she stopped running.

He took out their outfit for the day and he heard the water running which make him think she's taking her bath he shook his head at her eagerness to see her suprise.

He also went to take a shower in another room to save time he came back to the room all dressed up for the day and saw her struggling to put on her shorts that he picked out before.

He helped her with it and tie her hair into a pony tail and eat their breakfast. They went downstairs to find their family in the living room watching TV.

"Give me the remote idiot" Alisha said.

" No why would I" Aiden said glaring at her.

" Cause am the one who switch on the TV first" Alisha whined.

" I don't care" Aiden said rolling his eyes.

Alisha huffed and pout. Mia saw that and wiggle out of her father's arms and went towards Alisha and hugged her.

" Aunt Alisha don't be sad I know uncle Aiden is being a meanie we will punish him" she said kissing her cheeks.

Alisha smirk at the thought of punishing Aiden and she have the perfect idea.

She pout looking at Mia making a sad face" I know baby Aiden is such a big meanie, you're right he deserves a punishment" Aiden roll his eyes at her.

" Okay let me think" Mia said putting her hand on her chin thinking of the punishment he deserves.

" Seriously guys and what kind of punishment do I deserve for being a meanie cutie pie" he asked Mia playfully.

" I don't know aunt Alisha" she looked at her with hopeful eyes.

She smirks looking at Aiden who gave her a confused look " Aww baby doll how about no hugs and kisses for uncle Aiden from you" she said grinning.

" Yes" she said clapping her hands.

Aiden eyes widened and his jaw was about touch the ground" no you didn't" he said looking at his twin.

She smiles at him saying" oh I already did dear brother" kissing Mia's forehead.

" Cupcake you won't do that would you, you love me right please baby I need your warm hugs and kisses to survive. I don't know if I will even survive for a second without them and I will be so so sad because my baby won't give me kisses or hugs" he said pouting looking down.

Alex and Alisha roll their eyes hearing him.

" Can you guys quit this drama already, stop putting my princess in your game" Alex said.

Mia was looking at Aiden who's head was still down fiddling his fingers. Mia felt bad for punishing she doesn't want anyone to be sad because of her. Then she heard Aiden's fake snifflings she quickly went towards him and hug him kissing him all over his face making him smile.

" You gotta be kidding me, are you for real dude" Alisha said eyeing her twin.

" Oh hush you're just jealous because my baby loves me more than you" he said smirking.

" More than me my foot" she said rolling her eyes.

" Oh sis you are....." He started and their mom cut them off.

" Okay game over guys let's get going am tired of listening to your drama" she said.

" Grandma, grandpa" Mia said running towards them

" Pumpkin how are you doing" grandpa asked.

" Am good" she said smiling.

" Baby did you like your breakfast" grandma asked.

" Yes I loved it thank you grandma" she said hugging her.

" Okay let's get going we don't want to keep the princess waiting for her suprise" Alex said scooping her in his arms.

They all took what they wanted and went to the car and drove off. Mia being the most curious one out of them kept asking what's the suprise but the told her it won't be a surprise if they told her. She just pouted crossing her arms against her chest waiting for the suprise.

The car stopped and Mia couldn't her but gasped at the view beside her. It's a very beautiful amusement park that she have ever seen in her life.

She squealed hugging her dad" thank you papa I love it" he bend down a little to her eye level kissing her forehead lingering it she smiled.

" You're welcome baby you deserve more, okay go and play make friends also" he said ruffling her hair.

" Okay papa" she said looking at the kids playing some in the same, some on the swing, some playing tag and many more.

" Don't go where I can't see you princess stay where I can see you we will be sitting under that tree" he said pointing at a tree that his mom was putting a blanket under it.

She kissed his cheeks say" I will papa thank you" she holds Alisha's and Aiden's hands dragging them towards the swings to play.

Alex went to his parents who sat down chatting and glancing at his siblings who are busy playing tag with Mia, he smiled and took out his phone and starts playing some games on his phone that he download it for Mia.

" Hey Alex" he heard a voice that sounded familiar and looked up to see the owner of that voice.

" Damien what a surprise, how have you been doing" he said giving him a brotherly hug.

" Am good man, hey Mr and Mrs DeLuca" he greet them.

" Hello son it's been quite long that I have seen you" grandma said.

" Yeah I have been busy but I will try and visit soon" he said smiling.

" Well that's good keep up doing the good work Damien" grandpa said.

" I will sir" he said smiling.

" So how's your brat doing, don't tell me he's the one you brought here" Alex said him.

" Yep it's him he have been bugging me to take him out so here I am" he replied.

" So I heard from a little birdie that you have a daughter now" Damien teased.

" Yeah that my princess" he pointed towards Mia who Aiden was now pushing on a swing laughing.

" Wow she's cute" Damien said.

" I know right" he said smiling.

" Hey leo come here" Damien called his son who was running after some kids.

" Say hello to uncle Alex" he said.

Leo look at him amusingly" hey uncle lexxie" he said smiling sweetly at Alex

Alex groan at the nickname the brat gave him" hello there little devil" he said.

" Okay you can go back now" hearing that Leo ran back and continue playing.

" Your son haven't changed he's still the mischievous kid that I have ever met" Alex said.

" I know what can I do I just love him so much" Damien said.

" Yeah, yeah you love him whatever" Alex said giving him a glass of juice.

They sat down and started discuss about business. Damien is Alex's childhood friend and also his business partner he has a son Leonardo called Leo or Leon who's 6 years old.

After some time the twins came back looking exhausted and panting" bro you kid is so energetic" Aiden said gulping down a bottle of water.

" Don't even say it she's full of energy she's not even tired yet look at her" Alisha said looking at Mia who's on the slides sliding happily enjoying it.

" Whatever you guys are just getting old don't blame her she go that from me" Alex said as he stoop up with a bottle of water in his hand walking towards Mia.

Mia saw him and came running towards him she hugged his legs looking up at him smiling.

" Princess are you enjoying" he said her.

" Yes papa I am" she said.

" Ok here have some water" he said giving the bottle.

" Thank you papa" she said handing him back the bottle.

" Okay baby go play" he said kissing her temple.

She kissed his cheeks and ran back and continue playing.

Alex went back and sat down beside Damien " being soft are we" he said chuckling at Alex.

Alex roll his eyes and sip some water" she's an angel" he said.

They continue their chat. The twins are teasing each other while their parents are resting and cuddling each other.

" I think someone has a crush" Alisha said looking at Leo who was now beside Mia playing.

" Oh hell no" Alex said as he saw the way Leo was looking at Mia.

" Oh hell yeah" Damien teased playfully.

They came running towards their parents hand in hand giggling. Alex looked their joined hands he glared at Leo who doesn't even care about his surrounding he's just admiring the pretty girl who's holding his hand.

" Papa I thirsty" she said tugging on his arms.

" Okay princess and you have to eat something too okay baby" he said handling her a box of apple juice and some sandwiches.

He did the same to Leo. They ate and drank their juice. They rest a little bit and went off playing again. After half an hour Alex called them.

"Baby it's time to go" Alex said and she pout.

" Papa I don't wanna go am not tired yet" she said her lips starts to quiver.

Leo glared at Alex who looked suprise as to why he glared at him. Leo huffed at him and hug Mia.

" Princess we can come back another day buh now is getting late it's almost 5pm baby" he said Leo still hugging her as she sniffles.

" Shh Mia it's okay we can have a playdate tomorrow me and you I will come to your house tomorrow and we can even have a sleepover" Leo said cupping her face in his small hands.

" Really" she said.

" Yes, right uncle Alex" he said looking at him.

" Yes baby you guys can am sorry baby we can have ice cream right now if you want" Alex said glaring at Leo he was now jealous like seriously she just met him and now she's listening to him. How can he be jealous of a 6 years old God why him.

"Can Leon come too papa" she said beaming at him.

" Sure baby he can" he said kissing her forehead.

" Otay let's go" she said holding Leo's hand running towards the ice cream parlor near the park.

" What flavor do you want Mimi" Leo asked her.

" Strawberry" she said happily.

" Can we have a strawberry and vanilla ice cream" Leo said.

" Here you go kids" the girl said giving them their ice cream.

Alex was leaning against the door looking at them well he's glaring at Leo.

" Calm down bro" Aiden said smiling sweetly at him.

" Shut up" Alex said.

" Chill bro" Damien said.

" Hey kiddos it's time to go" Alex said.

" Papa here" she said handing him the rest of her half eaten ice cream.

He licked and kiss her cheeks" thank you baby" she blushed hugging his legs burying her head in her stomach.

" Aww she's so cute" Alisha said.

" Okay let's go baby" he said holding her hand.

They all went towards the car they were all ready to go. When Leo came towards them running with a stuffed animal in his hand.

He came walking towards Mia and hand her the stuffie, she smiled and hugged him.

" Thank you Leon" she said smiling.

" You're welcome Mimi" he hugged looking at Alex and smirks.

Alex gave him a confused look but what he did made Alex's eyes widened and his jaw was about to touch the ground.

Leo kissed her cheeks and ran towards his dad waving at her and smiling at Alex.

That little brat Alex said to himself.

" No he didn't" Alex said.

" Oh yes he did" Aiden said laughing at his brother.

" Aww they're so cute I totally ship them" Alisha said squealing.

" You gotta be kidding me are you for real guys" Alex said rolling his eyes as he looked at Mia who was now yawning as she was tired.

He scoops her in his arms" sleepy baby" he said.

" Yeah papa" she said nuzzling her face in his neck.

He kissed her forehead and went towards the car" okay sleep baby" he said as he settled down in the car.

Aiden was driving while Alisha was scrolling through her phone and Mia was on her father's lap napping.

Alex was thinking on how to get back at Leo tommorow because of what he did today. He can't believe that he's going to compete with a 6 years old God why him and he's even jealous of that little devil. He had an evil smile on his face as he thought of an idea on how to get back at Leo. He looks down at his princess who's cuddling him he kissed her forehead and hugged her smiling thinking how lucky he is for having her in his life.

Hello lovelies

What do you think about Leo? What do you think Alex gonna do to get back at Leo?

Any thoughts?

Hope you like this chapter.

Don't forget to vote comment and share if you're loving this story

Thank you for reading

CHAPTER 13

A lex pov:

I woke up to something heavy on my stomach and soft giggles. I opened my eyes to see my little princess sitting on my stomach giggling while playing with the rings on my fingers.

She was so engrossed in what she was doing that she didn't notice I was awake now. I gently wrap my arms around her taking her by suprise she squealed and buried her face in my chest.

I cooed at her kiss her forehead " good morning baby"

" Mowning papa" she said

" How did you sleep angel" I asked her.

" Fine" she mumbles in my neck

I chuckled at that" baby come let's freshen up and then we will go downstairs and have breakfast with grandma" i said picking her up and heading towards the washroom.

After finishing their morning routine they dressed up for the day and went downstairs for breakfast.

" Uncle Aiden good morning" my baby said running towards him.

Aiden who was laying lazily on the couch half asleep look at her mumbles the same. I roll my eyes, lazy ass he's not a morning person.

I entered the kitchen to meet my mom cooking I kiss her cheeks mumbling a good morning to her.

" How are you doing baby" she asked.

" I'm doing great" i said.

" Hey kiddo" I said to Alisha who just came in looking like a mess, her hair was all over the place with bags under her eyes.

" Had an interesting night I see" I said chuckling while ruffling her hair.

She smacked my hand away glaring at me then huffed and walk away drinking her orange juice.

" She's not a morning person you know that Alex" mom said laughing.

" I know they both are your devil twins" I said side hugging her

She pushed me away saying" don't you dare call my babies devils, they're are too adorable to be call devil"

I gave her the look that says 'are you for real' she just shoo me away to get out of her kitchen. But seriously she said her kitchen but is my house so it's basically my kitchen.

I went into the living room to find dad sitting on a couch reading a newspaper and a cup of coffee beside him. The devil twins who are chatting with my little princess who looks more energetic now than she is when she woke up.

" Good morning Dad" I said.

" Morning son, how was your night" he asked.

" It was good and yours" I said.

" Same as yours, hope you are ready for what's coming for you today" he said chuckling looking at my baby.

I raised an eyebrow at him and gave him a confused look" and what will that be dad" I asked.

" Are you forgetting the little playdate that you promised your daughter with her new friend yesterday" he said smirking.

" Argh!! Why did you have to remind me now about that little devil who's coming over today dad" I said glaring at him.

He just shrugged and points towards my princess" you have to worry about that there I think my little pumpkin has a little crush" he said.

" Oh hell no it's not happening not my innocent baby she can't have a crush on that boy. He's not even that cute or handsome whatever he's so ugly" I said walking towards my baby scooping her in my arms hugging her close to me buring my face in her hair.

Nuzzling into her neck she starts giggling saying" papa it tickles" I just smile kissing her forehead and sat down on a couch with her on my lap hugging her.

" Possessive much brother" Alisha said smirking.

" Oh sis I can't wait for today's playdate, I don't know if he's going to lock in a room or put a leash on her" Aiden said laughing.

A Smirking Alisha claps her hands excitedly saying" aww so today our dear big brother is going to burst from jealousy, because only yesterday he was fuming and I literally saw smoke coming out of his ears because of the tiny little innocent peck that little Leo gave our munchkin here"

" I wonder what will happen today" Aiden said to a fuming Alex.

" Shut up will you" I said hugging my baby closer to me who looks up at me smiling and kissed my jaw.

" Papa I love you" she said hugging me.

" I love you more princess" I said kissing her nose and she blushed hiding her beautiful face in my chest.

" Aww you guys are so cute, but seriously bro I totally ship them together they will be an adorable couple" Alisha said.

" I agree with you, though Leo is a good kid" Aiden said.

" I don't think so my princess is not going to date until she's 70 get that into your head" I said.

" Papa" my princess said.

" Yes baby" I said kissing her forehead.

" Can we go swimming in the pool today with Leon if he comes later" she said looking at me with her adorable blue eyes.

" Of course princess anything you want" I said.

She hugged me saying" thank you papa I love you"

" I love you too my little baby" I said hugging her closer.

" Oh my God I feel so unloved" Aiden said dramatically holding his heart feeling hurt.

" You're silly uncle Aiden" my baby said giggling and ran to him

She gave him a hug kiss him on the cheek and also went to Alisha and did the same to her say that she loves them too.

" Okay breakfast is ready everyone" mom said.

" Finally am starving" Aiden said and rush towards the dinning room.

Alisha roll her eyes saying" when are you not" following behind him.

" Shut up" he said to her.

" Let's go have some yummy breakfast baby" I took her in my arms and walk towards the dinning room too.

After having our breakfast we went into the garden to have a family time, we played some games to pass some time before the little devil arrives.

Gosh I don't know why my princess is so excited to meet him, she has been going on and on about how nice he is and he's going to be her best friend soon.

We were in the middle of chasing Mia when we heard the door bell ring well here goes nothing I mumble to myself.

Well I don't think so when my baby girl squealed and went towards the door saying Leon is here and she she ecstatic about it and can't wait to play with him again.

Alisha was the one who went after my princess to open the door for them.

On opening the door Leo entered his dad dropped him saying he was in a rush he was getting late for a meeting will be back later to pick him up. But the brat was looking here and there looking for someone obviously it's my baby that little devil. When his eyes landed on her he smiled and when towards her and hugged he looked up and saw me looking at them with a clenched jaw. That boy, that little brat, that little devil had the audacity to kiss my baby's cheeks again in front of him. He smirked at me and holds her hands and walks towards the garden like he wona damn lottery.

" Oh no he didn't do it again" Alisha said.

" Oh yeah he did" Aiden said laughing.

I glared at them went into the garden to found them playing on the swing. Oh it's game on little devil.

To be continued.....

Hello beautiful people

Am so sorry for not updating soon.

Hope you are loving this story so far. I can't wait for the next chapter.

To make up for not updating soon am going to do a double update today.

Don't forget to vote comment and share with your friends.

Thank you for reading.

CHAPTER 14

Alex sat down sipping his coffee watching his baby play with the brat. God why did they even choose that park if he knows that she's going to meet that brat there he wouldn't have choosen that park.

" Hey bro how is it going" Aiden said sitting next to him wiggling his eyebrows smirking.

" Shut up" Alex said glaring at him.

" Well I think it's going great because it have been an hour since he came here but I can see your baby asking for you. You know in a normal day if she doesn't see you for more than 15 minutes she start asking where's her papa but now I think you are gonna be replaced soon though" Aiden said chuckling.

" Well I don't think so, my princess can't replace me am telling you. Just wait and see she will start looking for me sooner or later. And about that brat am gonna show him that she wants me more than him" he said smiling.

" Argh whatever we shall see" Aiden said.

After 10 minutes Mia came running towards Alex and jump into his arms saying that she misses him and was hungry.

So he decided to give her a snack, the little devil came running behind them into the kitchen.

" Can I have some to uncle Lex.... um Alex" Leo said looking at him innocently.

" Um oh sure" Alex said.

" Here you go baby" he gave her some chocolate chip cookies and a cup of milk.

" Oh Leo we are out of cookies maybe you can have some biscuits" Alex said smiling sweetly at him.

" Um no thanks I will just have some orange juice if you don't mind please" he said.

" Leon you can have some of mine" Mia said offering him the cookies.

Leo looks at Alex smirking and said" thank you princess" he picked one and start munching on it.

Alex couldn't believe his eyes, he was suprise that she even offered him the damn cookies that she doesn't share it with anyone except me. Wow just wow she just met him yesterday and now she's sharing cookies with him.

" Here you go kids" I gave him a glass of orange juice.

" Thank you Uncle Alex" he said smiling.

"Baby do you wanna watch a movie with papa if you are done" Alex asked Mia who was buy stuffing her face with cookies.

" Sowwy papa Leon and I are gonna play some games on his iPad maybe later" she said smiling at him.

" Okay baby have fun" he said kissing her temple and went out of the kitchen.

Argh!!! Leon this Leon that gosh I don't like that kid at all now and the way he's being too close to his baby he can't wait for the day to end so that he could have his princess to himself after the little devil leaves. Little did he know what's going to come.

" Leon let's go to my playroom I wanna show you my stuffies" Mia said dragging Leo to her playroom.

She show him all her stuffie and her favorite/best friend penny. He just sat there looking at her babbling about them and smiling.

" Kids come down it's lunch time" grandma yells after some hours.

They rush downstairs and went into the dinning room giggling at each other.

" Baby" Alex said smiling at her.

" Yes papa"

" Did you have fun" he asked

" I did it was so fun, I showed Leon my stuffies and we both had tea party with them" she said excitedly.

" What about you Leo, are you liking it here so far" he asked him

" Uncle Alex am not liking it but am so loving it, it feels like am home" he said smiling looking at Mia

" Oh Leo it is your home and you are always welcome here" grandma said smiling.

" Thank you Mrs. DeLuca" he said.

" No you silly boy call me Amanda or grandma like Mia calls me" she said serving them some lunch

" Okay grandma" he said and starts to eat.

You gotta be kidding me Alex thought to himself my baby was not enough but now my mom too is now under his magical charms. We did they even see in this little devil to like his so much.

" Grandma can I have some apple juice please" Leo asked her politely.

" Sure you can" she said picking up the jug half filled with apple juice and pour it in a cup and gave him.

" Thank you" he said smiling at her

" You're welcome dear" she continue eating her lunch.

Alex just roll his eyes saying " mom can I have some too" he said looking at her she just huffed at him

" Serve yourself you have hands" she said not even sparing him a glance.

I couldn't believe his ears, he looked at her with wide eyes and a jaw that was about to touch the ground. His siblings snickered at him while Leo looks at him with an evil smile.

Alex just sulk down on his seat playing with his food. Mia saw everything and was sad because she saw how her papa was sulking and looking down on his plate. Mia doesn't want her dad to be sad she wants him to be always happy so with shaky hands.

With her shaky hand she pick up the jug with some difficulty and serve her papa some apple juice happily.

Alex cooed at her she's so cute" thank you so much baby, I love you" he said kissing her cheeks.

She beamed saying" you're welcome papa I love you too" and went back to continue eating her lunch.

Alex looked at Leo to see him staring at them he smirk and continue eating his food.

After having some lunch they went into the living room to watch a movie.

Everyone went at have a seat except the three which was Alex, Leo and Mia. Well Mia always sits on Alex's lap when watching movies they cuddle with each other that's why the did sit she was waiting for him to come so they could cuddle because he went to answer an important call.

Leo on the other hand was waiting for her to sit so that he could sit beside her but Mia had other plans.

Alex came back and he brought popcorn and chips for all of them he sat down and Mia immediately went towards him and sit on his lap happily putting her face in the crook of his neck sighing and mumbles 'papa'.He chuckled and kissed her forehead.

He looked at Leo who was still standing he smile evilly at him saying " Hey little come here" he said patting the empty couch beside him.

Leo huffs and sat down not without grabbing a bag of chips and start munching on it glaring at Alex from time to time.

Alex could feel his gaze on him from time to time and he was happy about it that he doesn't even need to do anything his princess is doing it all for him. He doesn't need to stress himself to think on how to get back at Leo, his baby is doing all the things he wants without asking. He sighs happily cuddling his sunshine more.

Half way into the movie Alex glance at Mia to see her sleeping on his chest her tiny fist are fisting his shirt.He saw it was around 2:30 in the afternoon it was way past her nap time cause she normally naps around 1:00pm. He gently carries her to their room and lay her down covering her with a blanket.

Turning he saw Leo behind him who was looking so exhausted and rubbing his eyes so cutely, Alex will have been in awe if he liked the little devil but no he doesn't he just raise an eyebrow at him.

" Uncle Lexxie can I nap here too I won't do anything I promise" he said looking at him with pleading eyes.

He would have melt but he didn't" no" he said sternly.

" Please uncle Alex I won't disturb her sleep I will just lay down beside her please" he said still pleading.

Alex sighs rolling his eyes" ohk but don't you dare disturb her and go lay down there quietly and sleep I will wake you guys up in a couple of hours. Because she wants to swim with you okay" he said

Leo went towards the bed and lay down beside her and close his eyes but not before holding her hand.

Alex saw what he did and huffs, he went downstairs to meet his siblings laying lazily on the couch watching a new movie now.

"God can't you guys sit properly on a couch like normal people" he said taking a seat beside Alisha.

" Nope we can't and stop comparing us with normal people, because you and me knows that we aren't normal right sis" Aiden said looking at Alisha.

" Speak for yourself dude" she scowled at him

Alex started laughing at a wide eye Aiden.

" Oh brother you just got burned by your own twin" he said holding his stomach.

" Oh shut up, weren't you the one who was pouting and sulking because your baby wasn't giving you some attention" Aiden said smirking.

" Oh hush you two are disturbing my peace" Alisha said.

" Oh really your peace" Aiden mocked

" You guy can't stand...." Alex started saying and was interrupt by a phone call.

The look at his phone and saw that it was Damien who was calling him (Leo's dad) he answer the call but what when heard from the other side made him want the ground to open up and swallow him. He ended the call saying it's okay.

" Oh you gotta be kidding me, it can't be for two freaking days God why" whisper yelled.

" What happened" Alisha asked.

" You can't believe what am gonna say right now, that little devil's father Damien just called me to ask a favour and you know what it was" Alisha shook her head " he freakings want to leave him here with us for 2 days you heard me 2 whole days with that brat oh my gosh" he said fuming.

" It's not a big deal you can take good care of him, you're so good with Mia" Alisha said chuckling.

" I know but you know how he gets on my nerves" Alex said.

" It will be alright we're with you bro" Aiden said patting his shoulder.

" I hope so" Alex mumbles and lay lazily sighing.

Thinking how he's going to survive 2 days with Leo. He mumbles some curses under his breath and continue watching the movie.

CHAPTER 15

A lex was laying down lazily on the couch taking a nap, while the twins are playing some games and eating snacks on the floor.

Little footsteps sounded through the living room head snaps the sound. The twin awe at her adorableness, Mia was walking towards her father rubbing her eyes with her tiny fist.

"Hey baby girl" Alisha cooed

" Hewo" Mia mumbles yawning.

" Awwn she's so cute" Aiden said as they continue to play.

Mia move towards her dad and tug onto his shirt but he didn't wake up he just stir in his sleep.

Mia huffed softly she climbed on top of him and lay on his chest. She nuzzle her face in the crook of his neck, clutching his shirt with her tiny fist.

"Papa" she said softly hugging him.

Alex felt something heavy on him so he started to open his eyes to see what is it but to his suprise it was his little bundle of joy. She's hugging like her life defend on him with her face in the crook of his neck. He starts to rub her back when he heard her call his name.

" Hey baby" he said kissing her hair.

" OMG am starting to get jealous, why can't I just go get my own kid" Aiden whined.

Alisha just roll her eyes at him while Alex just chuckled.

" My princess how was your nap" he asked her.

" Good papa" she replied.

" Okay, let's get some snacks into this little tummy of yours before dinner okay baby girl" he said ticking her tummy which made her burst into giggles.

" Otay" she said, he picked her up and when towards the kitchen for some snacks.

He gave her some snacks and got some for himself too and they went back to the living room. He sat her down on his lap hugging her from behind as she eats her snacks.

When they were done her gave some orange juice which she took gracefully with a big smile on her adorable face mumbling a thank you to him. While just smile and give a peck on the cheek.

" Hey Mia" Alex snaps his head towards the owner of the voice, he groan internally he has forgotten about the kid that's standing beside him.

"Hewo Leon, you want some" she said offering him her juice.

" No thanks, you drink it I will get one for myself" he said smiling at her.

" Here drink this" Alex offered his a bottle of water.

" Thank you Uncle Alex" he said.

" Hmm" Alex replied and continue typing on his phone.

Leo sat down on the floor beside Alex leg, as Mia saw that she started to wiggle out of her father arms so she could get down too.

Alex understood what she's trying to do he just roll his eyes and kiss her forehead before letting her go.

He groan internally thinking how he's gonna survive with this kid. And his princess on the other hand likes the kid so much, he doesn't even know what she saw in him to even like him. He's a little devil and a brat.

Mia sat down next to Leo and continue watching the cartoon on the TV, Leo turned his head towards Alex and smirk. Seriously Alex thought does he think he just won or something, but he did made Alex to gasp Leo sticks his tongue out at him then turn back him attention towards the TV.

The nerves of this kid Alex thought, Aiden snickered as he saw what Leo did to Alex.

" Dinner is ready lovelies" grandma announced from the dinning room.

They all got up and walks towards the dinning room to have their dinner.

During dinner Alex told Leo about his dad traveling and him staying with them for two days. On hearing that Mia squealed in happiness wiggling in her sleep trying to do a happy dance, she was so excited that Leo was going to stay with them. They are gonna have so much fun she thought. Leo on the other hand smiled at her, he just shrugged when Alex told him about it because he was used to it.

After dinner the went into the the garden to have some fresh air and have a family time before bed time.During the time the door bell rang Alex went to open the door, it was Leo's father's driver he came to drop Leo's things for him.

" Hello sir" the driver said.

" Hey Paul" Alex said smiling.

" Damien asked me to drop this for Leo and he said that he's sorry for the trouble" Paul said.

" No it's okay tell that he doesn't have to worry about him I got his back" Alex said and bid him goodbye.

He went into the garden and told them who it was and what he dropped. He saw his baby forcing her eyes not to close he just shake his head and towards her, he scoops into his arms he kissed her cheeks saying " time to go to bed baby"

" Nu uh" she said.

" But baby I can see you're so sleepy and it's even past your bed time" he cooed.

" Papa I wanna play more see am not sleepy" she said and a yawn escape her mouth.

He chuckled" yeah I can see that, but it's time for you sleep baby okay" he said rubbing her back.

" Papa you come too and sleep with Mia" she said softly.

" Okay baby am so tired too" he said faking a big yawn which made her burst into soft giggles.

" Otay papa and Leon too papa he will sleep with us, he told he can't sleep alone and he always sleeps with his papa like me" she said putting her head on his shoulder.

Alex looked at Leo who's also looking back at him waiting for him to answer her.

" Okay baby come Leo" he said.

The went into their bedroom and did their night routine, he changed her into her PJs and leo changes too and they climbed on to the bed to sleep.

Mia was in the middle of the two her head on her father's chest holding his arms as she falls into a deep slumber.

Alex kissed her forehead and said goodnight to Leo. As he was about to close his eyes he saw Leo trying to do what he just did. Oh hell no he's not kissing his baby again not in front of him. Alex glared at his covering Mia's face with his hands. Leo just smirk at him as he quickly took her hand in his and kissed it saying " goodnight uncle lexxie" and closes his eyes.

Seriously Alex thought this kid is going to be the dead of me. He sighs and close his eyes and slept.

THE NEXT DAY

Alex woke up before everyone he kissed his princess temple and went into the washroom to do his morning routine, after freshening up he went downstairs stair to make breakfast for everyone because he wants his mother to rest. She has been taking care of them so he's going to treat her and his baby their favorite breakfast which they both like.

After making breakfast he went upstairs to his room to find Mia waking up.

He takes her into his arms " good morning baby" he said kissing her cheeks.

" Good mowning papa" she said burying her face in his chest.

" Good morning uncle Alex" Leo said rubbing his eyes.

" Morning kid, hope you slept well?" Alex asked.

" Of course I did" he said.

" Leon" Mia waves at him smiling.

" Hey bunny, how are you doing this morning" leo said.

" Bunny?" Alex asked raising his eyebrow.

" Yeah it her new nickname" Leo said shrugging.

" Baby" Alex said looking at her, Mia was blushing buring her face in the the crook of his neck.

" Do my daughter looks like a bunny to you" he asked him.

Leo just shrugs saying" she cute so are bunny and it's my favorite animal"

Alex just huffed and went into the washroom with Mia in his arm, he made her do all her morning routine and came out with her and told leo to go in and do his own.

He pick up her clothes for her and dressed her up. Leo came out of the washroom and entered the closet to get dressed after a couple of minutes he came out full dressed.

They went downstairs to meet the rest of the family. The have their breakfast, Alex mother was so ecstatic when she saw what her son did and Mia was too she happily ate her breakfast wiggling happily on her seat.

Alex on the other her had a big smile on his face, smirking at a sulking Leo because all Mia's attention was on him giving him cute kisses now and then telling him how much she loves him. It's like she has forgotten about leo who was sulking beside her.

After breakfast Mia cling on to her papa she haven't let him out of her side. Alex who's loving all the attention would look at leo and smirk leo will just huffed at him.

Leo went towards them" Mia legs go and play" he said trying to hold her hand.

" Nu uh I wanna stay with papa" she said.

Leo looks taken aback and was now sad and walks away . Alex felt bad for him and said some soothing things into her ear explaining to her why Leo was here in the first place it was for her. Mia felt bad and ran towards Leo.

" Leo am sowwy" she said looking down at her little feet.

" It's okay Mia I understand" he said smiling at her.

Mia look up at him and smiled then hugged him.What she did next made Alex jaw touch the ground. She kissed on the cheek and starts blushing. Leo looks at Alex and smirk at him smiling like he won a freaking lottery.

Alex was starting to regret he did, he should have let him continue sulking and him cuddling with his baby but no he was the one that made her go to that little devil.

Leo hold her hand in his and ran towards her playroom to play.

Lunch time came they all went and have their lunch while chatting a little bit.They went into the living to watch a movie because the were all bored some minutes into the movie Alisha gave an idea of chilling next to the pool outside having some fun and eat some snacks.

" Pumpkin what to you wanna eat" grandpa asked her.

" P & j sandwich" she said happily.

" Okay baby girl p&j sandwich it is then" Alex said ruffling her hair.

" I wanna make it papa with Leon just the two of us for you guys" she beamed.

" Okay then grandma would show you how to make it ok but before then let change into your swimsuit" he said.

" Otay papa Leon let's go" she said holding Leo's hand.

After changing they went into the kitchen with grandma, she showed then how to make it then went out of the kitchen to meet the rest of them at the pool side.

" How's my little chef doing in here" Alex asked as he entered the kitchen.

" Good papa now go" she said Alex just laughed at her grabbing a bottle of water from the fridge. He stole a kiss from her which she whined and walked out.

When they were almost done with it Leo said something" Mia can one of uncle Alex sandwiches please" she nods

" Okay he's own it's gonna be special okay where make a smiley face on his own" he said

" Otay" she replied

" Take this to them while I make the last one for him Mia with the smiley face" he gave her plate full of sandwiches.

As he saw her walk out of the kitchen he smirked evilly and start doing his master piece. Mia came back and saw what he did with the sandwiches.

" Wow it's so pretty" said.

" Okay let's go" her gave her the plate.

The went out of the kitchen and go meet the rest of the family.

Mia walk happily towards her father, she pushed the plate towards his face " here papa Leon and I made this specially for you" she beamed happily.

" Aww thank you baby and Leo that's so sweet of you" he kissed her cheeks and nods at Leo.

They found a seat and sat down the starts to munch on their sandwiches, leo who was glance secretly at Alex who's eating it happily.

They were all engrossed in their food when they heard Alex coughing, his eyes has turned red Leo just looked at him and smiled wickedly at him when their eyes met. Alex looked at him with shocked eyes realization came to him that it was his doing well and not gonna make you win this he thought because his daughter was happy she made something for him with love and he's not gonna spoil it for him.

" Papa are you Otay" she asked him her voice sounded worried.

" Am good baby" he said and she smile kissing his cheeks

" All better" she said

" Thank you baby" he said sipping his apple juice to remove the horrible taste.

That's how he ate the rest of it gulping down his juice when he's finally done eating he let's out a big sigh.

Leo snorted seeing that, he smirk thinking of what he did.

FLASHBACK

After Mia went out of the kitchen Leo pour a small amount of jelly, ketchup and hot pepper sauce in a bowl and mixed them all together. He spread the mixture on the bread and smiled evilly thinking of Alex's reaction when he takes a bite out of this.

" And done" he said when he finished doing his master piece.

" Oh uncle Lexxie you're so gonna enjoy this, it's a pay back" he put away the bowl and wait for Mia to return.

Flashback ends.

After they were all done eating, Aiden was the first to jump into the pool followed by Alisha.Mia and Leo were just playing around the pool, Leo was chasing after her while she runs squealing everything he tries to catch her. Alex was not in the mood to swim today the was just near the pool looking at his twin siblings play in the water and his daughter playing happily.

Leo was chasing after her when he saw Alex was never the pool he smirk and ran after Mia who ran past her her fathet, Leo ran after and he pretends as if he's losing his balance when he reached Alex but he pushed him into the pool with full force.

Aiden gasped and starts to laugh at him follow by Alisha, Alex who came out to the surface of the water with a shocked face looking at Leo who was smirking at him and stick out his tongue at Alex and walks towards Mia.

Alex just groaned loudly making the twins laugh harder. Oh am gonna get you back little devil he thought to him himself getting out of the pool.

CHAPTER 16

"Hello everyone, who missed me?!" Someone said from the front door.

"Uncle Jammy" Mia said as she ran towards him.

"Oh isn't it my favorite niece" James said hugging her.

" Am your only niece silly uncle J" she said looking at him.

" Oh I know but you're still my favorite" he said kissing her forehead.

" Hey man" Alex said.

" Don't hey man me, it's all because of you am not having sometime to spend with my cute little niece here" he said tickling Mia which she burst into giggles.

Alex said rubbing the back of his neck nervously" i know I'm sorry buddy, but you know I want to spend some quality time with my baby girl here" he kissed her cheeks.

" It's alright I got your back, but you know the deal you coming back next week you know that right" James said glaring at him playfully.

" Yeah I know, don't worry about it but you're going to fill me in on how everything has been running in this past few weeks" Alex said.

James just shrugged saying" sure whatever".

They all went into the living room where the rest of the family members were watching a movie including Leo who was so engrossed in the movie, that he didn't noticed Mia who sat beside him was gone.

"Hey Amanda" James said as he sees her.

" Oh my, James where have you been a this while I have been asking Alex about but he keeps on saying your we're busy" she said smiling.

" Well yeah he's right I have been busy because of him" he said glaring at Alex who gave him a small smile.

" How's Melody doing" Gabriel asked him.

" She's doing great" James answered smiling.

" The two little brats how are you doing" he asked them.

" We're doing good as you can see" Alisha replied.

" Oh come on darling why are you being cold to him" Aiden said.

" Well did you not miss me when you haven't seen your favorite person" James said teasingly at her

She just roll her eyes saying" I don't miss you at all and you are not my favorite person keep on dreaming big guy"

" Well you kinda hurt my feelings Lee" James said putting his hand on his chest.

" Stop calling me with that stupid nickname Jam-Jam you know I hate it" she said glaring at him.

"What can I do the name suits you well Lee, and you are evening using that name Jam-Jam which you know a despise" he said sitting next to her.

" Okay enough is enough, I can't take it anymore guys can't you just have a casual conversation without being in each other's shoes" Amanda asked.

"Nope" they both replied while glaring at each other.

Alex just sigh saying" mom don't stress yourself please you know how they are with each other"

" I wonder how Melody fall in love with him, I think she needs a serious advise cause she has a bad taste in men" Alisha said smirking.

" Oh really then you should say that about yourself when that guy what's his name noa...." James started saying when she cover his mouth her hand. Her cheeks turn red.

" Okay please don't say anything now am sorry and I missed you so much my favorite person in the whole wide world" she said hugging him.

James looked at her shocked and then he smirked at her saying" aww Lee honey I know you missed you just couldn't admit it"

She just roll her eyes at him and huffed" whatever" she said.

"And how is this little guy here" James asked.

Alex just roll his eyes saying" don't tell me you don't remember him"

" Well I know who he is but what is he doing here, last time I check you guys don't get along well" James said smirking.

" Hello Uncle J" Leo said.

" Hey Leo how are you doing?" James asked.

" I'm doing good uncle J" he said smiling at him.

" Uncle Jammy he's my best friend" Mia said with a big smile on her face.

James pout saying" ohh I thought I was your best friend, I guess not anymore" looking down.

On seeing that Mia went towards him and hug him saying" you're my first best friend uncle Jammy, Mia loves you so much" kissing his cheeks.

" Aww my little munchkin I love you more my favorite niece" he said kissing her forehead.

" Let's go and play in the garden" Leon said as he holds her hand and ran towards the door that leads to the garden.

James and Alex went into his home office to discuss on how things are going in the company. James told all that has happened in fast few weeks and Alex has a proud smile on his face. Because he knows only James can handle his company when he's not around and he trust him with it.

Leon and Mia were playing in the garden and while the rest were either having a conversation or they are using their phone.

Lunchtime came and they all had their lunch together which everyone ate and complimented on the dishes. After lunch they thank Amanda (grandma) for the wonderful lunch. She was having a big smile on her face because of how happy she is that they loved her food.

Alex and James went into the living and put on a movie. In the middle of the movie James asked how his weeks have been. He told him all the happy moments he spend with his daughter and also the bad ones with Leo.

James burst out laughing when he heard what leo did to his friend, he was laughing so hard that tears came out of his eyes. While Alex was glaring at him saying it wasn't funny at all saying he will take his revenge too one day but that makes James even to laugh harder.

After sometime Mia came into the living room asking her dad and uncle to play with her and Leon in her playroom. Who can say no to her after seeing her beautiful blue eyes. They followed her to the playroom where they found Leon sitting in the middle of the room with lots of toys around him.

That's how they spend the day playing in the room, which later the twins joined them and play too.

Dinner time came they all had their dinner and James bid them all goodbye and went home. The rest went to their respective rooms. While Alex tuck in Mia and Leo in bed and lay beside Mia saying goodnight kissing her forehead. Like that he went into a deep slumber.

CHAPTER 17

It's been a week since Leo went back home and everything seems to be back to normal expect for the fact that Mia have been on Alex's back for the fast week about going to school (the one that Leo goes).

"Papa" Mia whined

'What is it now' he sighed and mumbled to himself

" Yes princess" he said smiling.

" Papa I wanna go to school like Leo does" she said looking at him with pleading eyes.

" And may I know why you wanna go there" he asked.

" Because I'm bored and I want to know and learn about new things and I wanna make new friends and I wan....." She started rambling.

" Okay, okay calm down baby girl" he said taking her in his arm and sat her down on his lap.

She hug him saying" please Papa I wanna go, see you don't have to worry about me being at home alone or making someone to look after me while you are at work. I would be in school learning new things instead of being here all alone dieing because of boredom" she said and dramatically fainted.

He shook his head at her silliness and tickles her" oh really your dieing because of boredom right baby".

She giggles saying" no Papa how can when I have you to entertain me" she tries to wink but blinked and he chuckled.

" Okay then as you wish baby" he said pecking her cheeks.

She squealed saying" really Papa you're gonna enroll me in school"

He nods " yes of course baby don't you wanna go anymore I can take what I said back" he smirked.

She shakes her head repeatedly" no Papa I wanna go, thank you Papa I love you" saying that she kissed his jaw.

He smiled at her gesture" I love you more". He kissed her forehead." okay sunshine what do you wanna eat for dinner" he asked.

" Pizza" she beamed

" Pizza it is then" that's how they spend their night laughing and enjoying the little moments they share together.

Before the night came to an end Alex made sure to inform his assistant do all the necessary things for his little girl that's needed to be done for her enrollment before end of the weekend.